SHADOW CAT AND THE SLOTH

A F.U.C. ACADEMY STORY

SCARLET FOX

ACKNOWLEDGMENTS

I would like to thank Eve for once again letting me write in her world. It is always a lot of fun! I can never say enough how much I appreciate her letting us do this.

I would like to thank Devin for all the amazing work with edits and suggestions. You help to shape the story and better it.

I would also like to thank Jessica Ripley for all the amazing behind-the-scenes work that she does, and especially for getting me back on track with the weekly word sprints. Whenever I am stuck—in any regard—I know I can count on her.

I also want to thank my other writing buddies who joined us to do word sprints over the winter. It really has helped keep me accountable to reach my writing goals.

I also want to thank my amazing partner, Brian, for always answering my random and bizarre questions to help me develop characters that are nothing like me.

I also want to thank Rebecca Poole for the amazing cover art!

As always, a big thank *you* for reading! I would not be here without my readers. I hope you enjoy!

~Scarlet

1

Ellie Talbot smiled widely in disbelief. It was a nervous smile that she had a habit of forming when uncomfortable. The excitement from moments ago dissolved into reluctance. The assignment she'd been patiently awaiting was here, except now it was all wrong. It was as if she'd ordered her favorite dish at a restaurant to find that it had been made with ingredients she was allergic to. But maybe she was over-reacting.

She had some hesitation in becoming a FUC cadet after the time she spent healing up in the dormitories of WANC, the Working and Administration Networking Core—main building of the academy. It was about a year ago that Ellie was rescued from a lab and moved into WANC. At first it was disorienting. But as she began adjusting to life as a shifter, Ellie met her best friend, Paige. It was a whole new chapter in the "post experimentation" book she kept in her mind.

Ellie had a tendency to file her life memories away like books. It helped her to keep track of when things happened as she pieced together her old life from faded images that would pop into her head randomly. The hardest part was figuring out the order of everything. That wasn't always clear. Whatever the scientists had done to her had left holes in her mind about what her former life had been like. The volume she called "pre-kidnapping" jumped around and sometimes didn't make sense. It was like recovering memories of a drunken blackout and trying to stitch them together into a coherent timeline.

The staff at WANC had been amazing through her difficult transition. Prior to being experimented on, Ellie had been a regular human. If you would have told pre-kidnapped Ellie that certain individuals could change into animals, she would have laughed in your face. It took post-experiment Ellie months to come to terms with not only what had happened to her but with what world she found herself in: the shifting world.

She had to accept that she could now turn into a black cat. What was harder to adjust to was refraining from chasing everything that moved. That and using a litterbox. Ellie now had a strong desire to find a place to dig a tiny hole when she had to go. It was embarrassing to admit, so she told no one.

Then there was the fact that sometimes she unconsciously batted at strings on her classmate's hoodies. Only after they gave her strange looks did Ellie even realize what she was doing. The urge was just so *intense* sometimes.

Once the WANC doctors and counselors had cleared Ellie's post-rescue mental and physical health, she decided she wanted to pay it forward, like Paige had. After being rehabilitated, her friend and fellow rescued experiment had become a counselor at FUCN'A—the Furry United Coalition Newbie Academy. But Ellie didn't know the first thing about psychotherapy. Instead, she decided to become a cadet and train to become an agent who would serve and protect the shifter community.

Not a day went by since she'd joined that she had regretted that decision.

Today, Ellie's technical training instructor, Grayson Stone, announced that they would spend the weekend doing survival training in the field. *That* was music to her ears. Excitement bubbled inside of her, and she could barely sit still. Get back into the wilderness? Heck yeah!

Her most vivid memories pre-kidnapping were of camping and hiking; just the thought of spending time outdoors spread a wide smile across her face. Every pre-kidnapping memory was special, but the ones where she could almost see the faces of her family were worth more than gold. Their essence was strongest in those wilderness images. What hurt was knowing that FUC hadn't been able to find an open missing person case matching her description. Either her family wasn't looking for her, or she didn't have any family left. Ellie wasn't sure she was ready to look into this further. What if her family was around but hadn't reported her missing? That would be too much to bear.

"No cell phones will be allowed on the trip. You will all be assigned partners for this task, and this list here is all the supplies we'll distribute to each team before we head out." Grayson stood at the front of the classroom and pointed to the whiteboard where the equipment list was scrawled out in his messy writing. He sniffed at the air and turned his head towards the door before focusing back on the classroom. Grayson seemed to never turn off his hound dog senses. He was always analyzing scents, being overly in tune with his surroundings. Ellie thought life like that would be overwhelming. Her slightly heightened sense of smell in human form was, at times, too much for her.

Grayson turned to his desk and picked up a notebook. In his monotone voice, he read off the list of pre-assigned partners. Ellie could hardly focus amid her excitement.

"Brett Kipp and Ellie Talbot."

Ellie heard the vinyl record screech in her mind as if someone had quickly yanked the needle off, scratching it. "B-Brett?" she asked, blinking in disbelief. Brett would be the partner she'd want if they were entering a modeling contest. But a survivalist assignment? No way. Brett could hardly get water out of a drinking fountain!

How in the world do they expect me to partner with him? Ellie thought, raising her hand.

"Yes." Grayson glanced up from his clipboard, raising an eyebrow.

"Do we get graded for how well we do?" she asked, her voice coming out an octave higher than usual.

"That is correct," Grayson said flatly, continuing with his list before Ellie had the chance to protest. So far, Ellie had excellent grades—which meant *everything* to her since she really had nothing else in her life she could control other than setting herself up for a future as a FUC agent. Partnering with Brett would not only change that, but it would be putting her life in danger during the training. It was true Brett was a FUC cadet, too, but his goal was to be support staff for the field agents. That didn't mesh at all with Ellie's dream of chasing down bad guys. And who knew what animal he changed into? Whatever it was, it probably wasn't too helpful in the field, based on his somewhat slow and often uncoordinated movements.

She glanced over to see the pencil Brett tapped nervously against his desk fly out of his hand and across the room. *I hope it's easier for him to keep a walking stick in his hands.* Ellie chewed on her lip. How would she keep her status as top cadet in her class with Brett as her partner? Disastrous scenarios filled her mind. Most of them ended with Brett somehow losing their gear or getting eaten by a bear. Ellie's excitement quickly deflated. She slumped back in her chair, watching Brett fumbling with the pencil as he tried to pick it up off the floor. He got it on the third try.

Ellie made a mental note: *Poor hand-eye coordination.* Maybe if she kept track of his faults, she could make up for them and still have a decent grade once the trip was done.

Once all the pairs were announced, Grayson explained the project in detail. "The pairs will be dropped off at various points in the wildlife refuge. You will all be given a map that shows how to get to your extraction point. Use your supplies wisely. Anyone who leaves early due to running out of food or water will fail the course."

Then Grayson made his rounds, passing out the maps among the cadets.

Ellie flicked her eyes back to Brett. She would have to be sure to watch his eating habits in the cafeteria. If there was any risk of him eating all their food, Ellie wanted to be prepared. Or at least aware of the risk. She was *not* failing this assignment.

"Now, get together with your partner to discuss your survival plan. Remember the list of supplies is on the board. You are allowed to bring anything extra you feel you may need. Just remember what you bring in you have to carry out." Grayson pointed to the board as a reminder as he observed the class beginning to greet their respective partners.

Maybe it won't be as bad as I think, Ellie thought as she got up from her chair, pulling it behind her as she crossed the room toward Brett's desk. Shadows rolled off of her as she moved toward him. She had *almost* gotten used to that side effect of the experimentation. Aside from being turned into a shifter, she had that new ability as well. It had something to do with dark matter and light bending.

A team of scientists had tried to explain it to Ellie when she was first rescued and studied in the hospital section of WANC. They could not fully define it to her in a way that made sense. She just knew that if she focused on the tingling sensation in her body and willed it to vibrate differently, she could bend light around her body and disappear. Kind of. She was still there, but no one could see her. Being invisible when she wanted, *that* was pretty cool. Maybe not worth the missing memories of pre-kidnapped Ellie, but she tried to make the best of it.

When she wasn't bending light around her,

shadows flowed from her as she moved. The reason the scientists gave her for that made less sense and gave her an hour-long headache when she tried to process it. It was much easier to tell people "it's above my paygrade" if they asked. In fact, that is exactly what she told Paige the day they first met.

Brett gave a shy wave from across the room, not fully extending his fingers when he made eye contact. Ellie sighed, dragging her chair over to his desk and plopping down, causing dark shadows to roll off of her with the quick motion. It was easier for her to control the dark matter when she moved slowly, but with fast movements, it was like a cloud of inky dusk surrounded her. Just another aspect of her abilities that the doctors at WANC didn't fully understand the purpose of.

"Hey." Brett's soft voice could hardly be heard above the muttering of the rest of the class, but his clear hazel eyes danced as he flashed his dazzling smile at her. "I can't *believe* I am partnered with you!"

"What do you mean?" Ellie asked. As far as she knew, she wasn't a celebrity among the cadets.

"You are one of the best in this class! You seem to know every answer to the questions Grayson asks. Plus, you are super nice." Just as she'd felt moments before the partners were announced, Brett was bubbling with enthusiasm. His smile could light up the darkest of days, and she couldn't believe she was able to make such an attractive man so excited to partner with her.

I am *nice,* Ellie reminded herself. Maybe she was judging Brett too harshly. A warm blush rose in her cheeks at the thought. She was embarrassed of herself for being so judgy.

"Thanks," she said, returning his smile before spreading her map out on his desk. "What are you thinking about a plan?"

"Plan?" Brett looked at her, curving up one of his thick brown brows.

Ellie's chest tightened, and she took a deep breath, calming her body from the anxiety she had about being seen as the best in this class—and all the expectations that were put upon her for it.

"We need to plan out where we should camp and how to use our supplies wisely," she explained. Ellie always needed a strategy. Even if it was as simple as what chores she wanted to get done during the day.

Brett nodded, flicking his eyes to the map. "Right…" His voice sounded so soft and unsure that, for a moment, Ellie forgot about the grades and suddenly felt a need to protect. *Maybe it won't be so bad. Maybe he just needs a good partner.*

"Have you been camping before?" she asked after watching his eyes bounce around their map. His silence was gnawing inside of her. She needed to know how much Brett knew about the wilderness.

"No." Brett didn't look up from studying the map.

Ellie was glad he didn't see her face, feeling that there must have been a look of judgment there. "I have always wanted to, though."

"Well, now's your chance. Good enough a time to start as ever." She delivered the lines through gritted teeth, trying to remind herself, *Be nice! Be nice!*

He looked up to the board with the list of supplies behind her. "Should we start with the supply list? How do you think we should split them up in case we get separated?"

"What? Why would we get separated?" The fact that he jumped straight from looking at the map to thinking about supplies and the possibility of losing each other in the woods had Ellie returning to her assessment that Brett was hardly prepared for their task. She regarded him with wide eyes, hoping he had an explanation.

Brett pointed to the map. "It looks like our path is along this river." His finger traced the red line of their trail along the blue vein of the water. "What if one of us falls in?"

The cat inside of her hissed, and she shot her hand up while scanning the room for Grayson. Ellie had been so stuck on trying to figure out how Brett had gone through his life this long without ever camping that she hadn't bothered to look at the map herself. Now, on top of an incompetent partner, she had to worry about *water?*

She *hated* getting even her feet wet. Not just now

but back when she was still human, too. Ellie had one strong pre-experimentation memory of stepping into a puddle on her way to school and having to sit most of the day with a wet sneaker. To this day, the second her socks get saturated, she was miserable. Especially if she was stuck in a scenario where she couldn't remove them.

Now that her regular distaste for water was combined with cat instincts, she hated even the *idea* of uncontrolled water. Showers, sure. Pools, not really her thing, but at least she could choose to jump in or not. A wild river? No. No way.

Grayson nodded her way, beckoning her to ask her question from across the room.

"Our trail is along the river," she said, voice strained. Her mind was short-circuiting, barely able to string together words. Ellie still struggled with her new urges. Turning into a cat shifter so late in life had not been an easy adjustment. The others, who'd been born shifters, had their entire lifetime to get used to their animal side. She'd only had over a year.

"Yes," Grayson replied. "Some groups will need to travel by water. You'll find rafts you can use along the way."

"But this isn't a small little lazy river!" Ellie protested. "It's a big Canadian one with rushing water and rocks and… and…"

"Rapids, yes," Grayson said as though it were of

no consequence before turning to answer another classmate's question.

Ellie felt the walls closing in on her. There was no way she could avoid getting wet if they were boating down rapids. This wasn't fair. The first opportunity to go camping as a shifter, and she had to go *rafting*!

"So… splitting the supplies… How do you want to do that?" Brett's downturned eyes were wide, reminding Ellie of a lost puppy. He was oblivious to the panic going on inside of her.

Ellie swallowed, shutting her eyes to try to center herself and get her pussy back under control. She sucked in a deep breath through her nose and blew it out through her mouth forcefully, focusing on the sensation and sound. It was a trick Paige had taught her so she could ground herself—useful when distracting herself from chasing balls of yarn when she walked by the hobby shop in town. Unfortunately, it wasn't making a lick of difference now. But she'd have to force herself to focus and move on.

"We need to evenly split the food. And I would like all the tuna pouches if you don't mind." Ellie exhaled with a heavy sigh. "And maybe we should see how far we can make it each day without needing a break. I am sure some parts of the rapids are worse than others, so we can plan that as we go. We just have to be mindful of how much daylight is left in the day."

Things felt better now. Ellie liked solving problems, and now she was working her way through this one. Their trip would be like a puzzle, and making it through without getting soaked was just a piece that she had to be prepared for. Maybe she could still enjoy herself. *I can do this*, she reassured herself.

Brett pressed his lips together, nodding. "That makes sense to me."

He squinted as he studied the map, running his long fingers through his wavy brown hair as he did so. Ellie smiled, despite everything else going on. Brett had such a carefree demeanor, combined with some Harry Styles-type good looks. Brett had to know this would be a difficult journey, yet he remained focused and unflappable.

Part of Ellie was angry and disappointed in herself. Brett was too nice to be the focus of her ire. It wasn't his fault he was her partner. It was unfair of her to take that out of him. She felt guilty for the thoughts she had earlier, assuming he would make her get a bad grade on this assignment. Maybe he wasn't going to be as bad of a partner as she initially thought.

Besides, she was the one panicking about the river. Here she'd thought Brett would be the problem, but maybe *she* would be the one to ruin the assignment.

"Wait," Brett said suddenly, snapping Ellie out of her ruminations. "Why do we have to be mindful of the daylight?"

Ellie chewed her lip, pausing before she answered so she could choose her words wisely. She was *nice,* after all. Brett had reminded her of that. *Be nice.* "Because it's no fun trying to pitch a tent in darkness. If we stop too late in the day, it will be hard to find a suitable site to camp."

She tried to give her best smile, but she could only manage to pull up one corner of her lip for a second. Anxiety had fully extinguished all her optimism and excitement about the assignment. Would she have to teach Brett every step of the way? How much would that slow her down? Forget her grade; what if they couldn't make it to the extraction point on time?

What if she got *wet*?

Ellie's stomach was in knots, and her mind was almost out of control at this point. She envisioned herself as a cat clawing the raft to pieces in an attempt to stay out of the water. Maybe it was silly to fear that she wouldn't be able to keep her shit together in her human form, but Ellie also knew how she reacted to rain as a cat. It wasn't pretty.

"What do you shift into?" Brett's warm voice somehow soothed her anxiety.

"A cat," she replied quickly, ready for him to share his animal too.

"Oh. That explains the look on your face. You look terrified." His words seemed sincere, and she almost thought that he sounded as if he felt bad for her. *Him? Feel bad for* me?

"I am good at camping and hiking, though," she added, not wanting the pity from the man who'd never been camping before. She looked down at the blue squiggle on the map that symbolized the river they would be trekking down, still waiting for him to share his animal side. She almost didn't want to know the answer. What if he was another animal that hated getting wet? Maybe they could just spend all their time in their human forms and avoid water if necessary. Finally, she had to ask, "You don't change into a cat, do you?"

"No." Brett shook his head. "I do not shift into a cat."

Ellie let out a sigh of relief. She could let go of the picture of two wet cats stuck in a raft. That sounded like a shifter horror flick.

"I'm a sloth." A shy smile spread slowly across Brett's freckled face.

Her heart sank. *Shit. I am going to be a cat in water with a slow-as-molasses sloth on a timed assignment. We are so fucked.*

Sometimes being a shifter was fun, but in circumstances like this, it was stressful! Ellie used to love outdoor activities. Or at least, she thought she did. Images of canoe trips were part of her pre-experiment memories. Those memories always came with a sense of peace, so she assumed she used to enjoy water—at least as long as her shoes didn't get waterlogged. But now, the cat inside of her shrunk at the thought of being anywhere near it.

"What's wrong?" Brett asked, his brows furrowed in concern.

Ellie didn't want to tell him her worries about him slowing her down, so she gave him half of the truth. "My cat side isn't a fan of water."

She hunched her back, feeling slightly defeated before the assignment even began. Fears of wet feet and clothes filled her mind. Worse, what if she freaked out in the raft and caused them to flip? Or the rapids popped their boat? Then she'd be wet for sure. The whole thing made her uneasy and gnawed at her stomach. Ellie chewed on her lip as more scenarios flooded her brain.

Brett puffed up his chest. "I will do my best to keep you dry."

A slow smile spread across Ellie's face, tugging at the corners of her mouth. *What a sweet thing to say*. He was a chivalrous knight at her service. "Thanks," she said softly as her anxiety began to melt away. She knew it was probably impossible to stay dry on the trip, but something about Brett's confidence was soothing. Maybe the assignment would be better than she initially thought. The world didn't end every time a cat got wet. Ellie had to slow her roll and put everything back in perspective.

If only her anxiety would agree with her and take a backseat on this one. Unfortunately, the FUC scientists had yet to come up with a cure for undesirable nerves, so it would just take practice and courage to overcome it.

"But you may have to help me stay awake," Brett said, stretching back into a yawn. "Sloths like to sleep a lot!"

Damn it. Ellie's eyes widened in horror. Yep, her first thought was right. This assignment was going to be a struggle for the both of them.

The outdoors wasn't something that Brett was a pro at, which probably wasn't a surprise to any of his classmates. He had never been camping growing up, and when he found himself in a forest, he generally wanted to climb into the boughs of a tree and take a nap. He couldn't help it. His sloth side enjoyed sleeping.

Brett couldn't believe his ears when Grayson read the groups out. Brett was partnered with Ellie Talbot, the smartest cadet in his class, for the biggest assignment yet. Ellie was the single person who seemed to have an exceptionally vast knowledge of all things survival. She was the one who knew all the answers to any questions their instructors lobbed at them, from naming edible plants in the region to listing various methods to start a fire. In contrast, Brett had to work hard at his grade. This was not an easy class for him.

He didn't know Ellie that well outside of the classroom, but he'd been drawn to her since the first time he laid eyes on her. With those strange shadows rolling off her at all times, others might find her creepy, but Brett thought she was unique.

And quite beautiful.

Plus, she was nice, always having a smile for whoever she passed in the hallways. Brett had wanted to get to know her better but hadn't yet found the courage to do more than just smile or wave from a distance. Now it would all change. This assignment gave him the opportunity to finally talk to Ellie.

When Ellie's face dropped after they started working on their plan, it saddened him. She was always so cheerful, so it was difficult to see her worried. Even her shadows appeared bummed out as they dropped off of her arms as she slumped back into the chair. That was when Brett blurted out, "I will do my best to keep you dry," like some dork. The second the words were out of his mouth, Brett regretted them, especially when Ellie gave a weak smile before chewing on her lip again.

He mentally slapped himself on the forehead. The words he uttered were cringe-worthy, and he found himself shrinking back from Ellie, his confidence shrinking too. He might as well get a giant "L" tattooed on his forehead.

Getting tongue-tied around women he found attractive was nothing new. It was why he generally kept to himself and why it had been quite some time since Brett had been on a date. In fact, he couldn't remember the last time. Not that he dared think Ellie would be interested in dating him. The very idea left his stomach tied in knots.

After notifying Ellie of sloth sleeping habits and watching alarm fill her eyes, Brett decided to stop talking about himself and focus back on the assignment. He wished he could pop all of his words back into his mouth and erase them from existence. He was trying to be reassuring to decrease her anxiety and not increase it, but so far, he was failing, and the voice in the back of his mind kept repeating, *You don't belong here.* Some days he really wondered if he deserved to be a FUC cadet.

Brett racked his brain for something helpful to say. Anything that would be productive for planning and wouldn't leave him feeling like a waste of space. The silence between them drew on awkwardly. He shifted in his seat and glanced up at the clock on the wall behind Grayson before he finally settled on, "Do you think there will be any parts that we will have to carry the raft through? I saw that in a movie once."

Ellie's blue eyes appeared to be studying his face.

The seconds felt like minutes before she replied, "I have no idea."

Her words were flat, not Ellie's usual bouncy tone she had when answering questions in class. She frequently talked with a smile on her face, but now there was hardly the hint of one. Was it all because of her fear of the water?

Or was it because of him? He knew that the other cadets saw him as a geek who wanted to remain indoors instead of being out in the field like the other agents. While it was true that he wanted a position where he would spend most of his time on the computer, he hoped that this didn't taint how Ellie saw him as a partner for an outdoor assignment.

"I have strengths, too," Brett blurted out, trying to block out the fear of judgment and rejection that was creeping up. They were limbs of a kraken, threatening to pull him back under the waves of self-doubt.

"What?" Ellie blinked at him, the light shining off of her black, curled lashes. She raised an eyebrow in confusion, cocking her head sideways as if she missed something. A semi-circle of darkness ebbed off of her in a swirling flourish. That was something Brett would have to get used to while working with Ellie. He'd noticed her shadows in passing, but up close was a different story. They seemed to take on a life of their own.

Brett supposed he did confuse Ellie, as the conversation he was having had previously occurred with himself inside his head. He had always felt self-conscious about being a sloth shifter, starting way back when he was the last kid picked in gym class growing up, so activities like survival training made his insecurities creep up.

"Uhh…" Brett flicked the edges of the laminated map as he chose his next words carefully. "It may not sound like a sloth would make a good partner on a boating expedition, but sloths are actually great swimmers—we're even capable of holding our breaths up to forty minutes!" Brett was glad to brag about his animal whenever he was given a chance. There was way more to sloths than just how slow they moved or how cute their smiles were.

"I didn't know that." Her words sounded sincere, and he thought it seemed like she might have relaxed a bit, but she still wasn't acting like her usual confident self.

"Not a lot of people do," he replied. "Even in the shifter community. Sloths aren't very common. We're even less common among the FUCN'A cadets."

Brett offered the information in hopes that Ellie would feel open about sharing her own story with him. He had heard that she came to the Academy originally as a rescue who'd formerly been a human. The very idea boggled his mind. How difficult a transition that must have been! But he also felt it was rude to ask. It felt too personal.

Ellie smirked. "I don't think I have ever seen a cat

swim. I hope I don't make a *terrible* partner." She sighed and hung her head as she played with the hem of her shirt.

Brett couldn't believe that Elle could think something like that. How could she when she'd clearly demonstrated that she was on track to be an excellent field agent? If Brett had to remind her of that to melt her fears of the river, he would.

"Are you kidding?" Brett asked, his voice bright, hoping to coax Ellie's mood back to the positive side. "You have gotten top scores this entire semester. There is no way you could be a bad partner." When Grayson wasn't looking, he pulled out his cell phone. "And there's plenty of videos of cats, big and small, playing in water or swimming."

Ellie peered over his arm, watching the video montage of tigers wrestling in a stream and house cats swimming quite happily in bathtubs. "I had no idea that other cats liked water."

Brett hoped his videos boosted her confidence. Maybe things could change for her, and she could learn to enjoy it.

Before Brett could gush about all the things he admired about Ellie, Grayson announced, "Class is concluded for today. Don't forget to meet in the parking lot Friday for your ride to the drop-off points. Show up with enough time to sort your supplies and pack your bags. And dress appropriately for the trip. You are allowed to pack whatever clothes you would like, but be mindful that you have to carry whatever you bring with you."

Brett swallowed hard. He wasn't sure if he had any appropriate clothes for the trip. Aside from his supplied uniforms, he generally wore sweaters and khakis in his spare time. He almost asked Ellie if she thought he needed hiking boots for this assignment but decided to keep his mouth shut. He didn't want to risk embarrassment again.

"See you Friday morning," was all he muttered instead. Brett sighed as Ellie got up from her chair and left the classroom. He had so much to prepare for. He didn't want to let his partner down.

2
———

"What do you mean you think you're going to *fail?*" Paige, Ellie's best friend, asked with a shriek after swallowing her coffee. Her brows furrowed as if she didn't believe a word of what Ellie was saying. With how loud Paige was, Ellie was surprised that the other customers in the coffee shop didn't look their way, but they went along with their conversations without interruption.

"I just have a bad feeling about this assignment, is all." Ellie picked at the rim of her paper coffee cup. The fear of failure would not leave her alone, keeping her up at night for so long that she finally texted Paige to ask if they could meet for coffee. Her friend knew the right things to say to ease Ellie's mind.

"If you keep that up, your coffee will leak out. No one wants that," Paige joked, pulling Ellie's fingers away from the seam of the cup after more pieces of the container fell to the tabletop like fresh snow. "Do you want to talk more about it?"

"I just…" Ellie sighed, sitting back in her chair in the café. She didn't know where to begin. There were her fears about her shifter animal's reaction to water in addition to the worries about Brett's performance. "I just don't know how we can be successful with our assignment."

"Why do you think that?" Paige's voice was soft. It was her therapy voice. Ellie could always notice the adjustment in her friend when she went into "work mode."

"At first, I was so excited." The words tumbled out of Ellie's mouth. "The few memories of my human life that were most vivid were of camping and being outdoors. But this is a rafting trip, and my cat is losing her shit!"

Paige giggled. "What's wrong? You don't want a wet pussy?"

"I'm serious!" Ellie spat out, playfully slapping her friend on the shoulder. "This is nothing to joke about." She pursed her lips out in a pout, sighing heavily. The situation felt like the end of the world to her, and she couldn't explain why. Sure, the assignment was important, and failure was not an option, but it wasn't like the Academy instructors would just leave them out there if they didn't check back in time, right?

"Okay… Okay…" Paige bit her lip in an attempt to

keep her laughter in. She closed her eyes and exhaled through tight lips. When her eyes fluttered back open, she asked, "So, there's the rafting aspect, but that's not all. What else is bothering you?"

Paige had the uncanny ability to sniff out fear like a hound dog. Besides, she knew that when it came to Ellie, it took a lot to get her so worked up, and in that case, there were usually a ton of anxious thoughts running through her mind at once. It didn't happen often, but in Ellie's case, when it rained, it poured.

Ellie took a deep breath before admitting, "My partner is a sloth."

"So?"

"So, he's slow and sleepy and completely ill-equipped to survive in the wilderness himself, let alone save me if my cat freaks out at the river!"

"Really?" Paige asked with a smirk. "I'm a tiger. Do you see me pouncing on and eating random people?"

"No…"

"You, being a new shifter, might have some issues controlling your cat instinct sometimes, but natural shifters can generally manage their animal side. Just because your partner is a sloth doesn't mean that he will be slow. Does he walk slowly in human form?"

"No," Ellie said, processing Paige's words. "You mean, it's not normal that I sometimes want to dig a hole outside to pee in instead of using the washroom?" She admitted her most embarrassing secret to Paige, fearing that one day the urge would be too strong.

"Good thing you're camping. Isn't that what you'll have to do?" Paige quipped with a smirk.

Ellie couldn't help but giggle. "I am being *serious*! My point is that what if he has some urges that he *can't* control? And what if those impulses ruin my final grade for the course? Or my fears of water create a..."

"A *cat*-astrophe?" Paige interrupted. She bit her lip, trying to keep her laughter in, but it bubbled up regardless. Her shoulders bounced as it spurted from her lips in waves.

Ellie cocked her head to the side. "I am glad you are finding this so amusing." She watched the steam swirl out of the lid of her coffee before deciding to take a sip. Its warmth was comforting. Ellie assumed there must be a happy human memory attached to the drink, but she was never able to access it. As annoying as that was, she was just glad for the content feeling that accompanied slurping the bitter brew.

"Ellie," Paige said in a warm, sincere tone. "It will be okay. You have to repeat that to yourself because if you go into this assignment only thinking of all the wrong that can happen, you might create a self-fulfilling prophecy."

Paige was right. If Ellie focused on what could go wrong, she would be setting herself up for failure. She would have to try to ignore the stress of being near the water. Besides, Ellie knew her way around a campsite pretty well. She was knowledgeable about what in the wild she could eat, what plants were useful, and which ones were poisonous, among other things. That was what this assignment was about. Putting those skills to use.

The edges of Ellie's lips curved up into a grin. Her earlier anxiety melted away with her return of confidence. "Thank you." The tension eased almost immediately. She could do this. And it could be a lot of fun.

"What else is your partner like?" Paige asked, interrupting Ellie's thoughts. "Aside from being a sloth?"

Ellie rubbed at her chin. In class, she had only focused on Brett's faults as a woodsman. She forgot about who he really was. "Well..." Ellie started, searching for what she knew about him outside of that class. "He always smiles or says hello to me." It wasn't much, but it was a start.

"So... he's not a dick," Paige summed up with a toothy grin. "That's good in a partner. You could be paired up with someone who drives you crazy."

Ellie nodded as she giggled. "Good point! At least my partner is sweet and thoughtful. Not great in the woods, from what I gather, but it sounds like he hasn't had the chance to try yet. Like, he has *never* been camping."

"Really?" Paige drummed her fingers on the table. "So… there's really no evidence to show that he won't be a good partner."

"Well… he seems best at computers," Ellie said with a shrug.

"So?" Paige laughed defiantly. "Plenty of nerdy people are great outdoors. I bet if you give him a chance, he will surprise you."

Paige gave a wide reassuring smile, making Ellie so glad they decided to meet for coffee. "You always know how to make me feel better, especially when it feels like my world is crashing down on me. And when it comes to school and concern about my grades, I feel that way frequently. I just can't help it."

"Any ideas why that might be?" Paige prompted, still using her therapist voice.

Ellie took a deep breath, mentally flipping through her pre-kidnapping book of memories. "Middle school. I'm trying to hide a test where I scored a ninety-two. I can still feel the embarrass-ment of that day nipping at me."

"Is there anything else? Your parents' reaction?"

Ellie shook her head. "No, I only remember *me* being devastated by the grade. I know I put way too much pressure on myself, but it's such a hard habit to break. Why do you think I get so stressed out about it?" The question weighed heavy on her mind and was one more aspect of not remembering her past that frustrated her. It was like trying to complete a paint-by-number with a quarter of the colors you needed to see the full picture.

Paige sipped her coffee with a faraway look in her eyes. "I'd gather you were probably always this way. Things that people feel strongly about are easiest to remember or feel."

Ellie leaned forward, resting her chin in her hands. The patchwork of her former life was an exasperating mystery. How could someone learn to be themselves again without remembering most of their past experiences? Ellie was still getting the hang of being a shifter, but she didn't know if she'd ever become used to not having her memories.

As if knowing the internal struggle in her friend, Paige said, "Just be patient with yourself. It takes time to heal."

Ellie stared out the window of the coffee shop, watching others on the street chat and laugh as they passed, as if they didn't have a care in the world. "I just need to stop getting stuck in my head."

"That couldn't hurt."

"Sometimes, I don't know if I rushed into being a cadet before I was ready. How did you know you were ready to move on?" Ellie asked, wondering how Paige discerned when she no longer needed to be a patient healing in WANC and could get a fresh start at life.

Paige squinted deep in thought. "I think if we keep putting something off until we feel ready, we will never accomplish anything."

"When did you become such a sage?" Ellie quipped, though she couldn't deny that her friend had a point. If Ellie had remained in the dorms as a rescued experiment instead of joining the Academy, she would never know that she had the courage to try to be more, to find her place in this new world. The shifter world.

Brett found himself browsing through the small outdoors section of a store the next town over. After perusing through his closet, he confirmed that there were no suitable garments for this trip. He studied the weather reports for the weekend. All said that it should be beautiful early summer weather, albeit cooler at night.

One forecast mentioned possible rain—thunderstorms to be exact—and Brett hoped that was incorrect, considering how fearful Ellie was of getting wet. He wondered why their group had specifically been assigned to an area that included rafting. Sure, Grayson seemed like a "tough love" kind of instructor, but wouldn't he have informed them if this was an intentional "face your fears" kind of mission?

If it was, then what fear was Brett supposed to be facing? Talking to Ellie, the cadet he'd secretly had a crush on?

He pushed that thought out of his head. He hadn't even admitted to himself that he admired the shadow cat. That was ridiculous. He could hardly talk to her, let alone ask her out.

After riffling through the hangers on a rack, Brett chose some clothing that he could layer. It seemed sensible to choose something that could be removed later if needed, and he hoped that thinking ahead would give him points toward being prepared.

He certainly had no idea how well he'd score on handling the unexpected.

Before realizing that they were assigned to the river, he had hoped his journey would take him through the forest. His sloth enjoyed that. He wouldn't have needed a tent if he were able to snuggle into the welcoming branches of a tree. A warm smile spread across his face just thinking of it. He had been so busy with his various courses he hardly had time to relax. Brett often worked on his assignments while staring longingly out the window at the waiting woods on the edge of campus.

Some days it was difficult to stay the diligent student, but Brett felt he was always behind the other cadets. Most of them were fluid in their movements during tactical training, while he nearly tripped over his own feet or rolled right when he should have ducked left. It wasn't like he had a choice, though. FUCN'A didn't have different training for field agents versus tech agents. Cadets had to get through the initial training to earn their place in a specialist apprenticeship.

Knowing his deficits, Brett decided to work that much harder. He spent his nights on the obstacle course or the gym, working on coordinating his moves. On the nights his body ached, he read textbooks and field manuals instead. When his body needed a break, he worked his mind harder. Regardless of the extra work he put into being a cadet, Brett continued to feel behind the eight ball. That was his reason for taking survival training as one of his electives. Brett knew that it would give him the opportunity to prove to himself that he could be a well-rounded FUC agent.

After scooping up shirts with a variety of thicknesses and sleeve lengths, he moved on to the shoe section to find the best pair of boots. They all looked the same to him. He decided on a pair that boasted of being waterproof and light in weight.

His mind drifted back to Ellie. He did not want to let her down. Originally this class was to prove to himself what his abilities were, but now he wanted to show her that he was an asset. So much so that he'd spent last night studying and memorizing the map.

He was going to demonstrate to his colleagues—and himself—that he would be a great FUC agent.

He waltzed up to the register with a triumphant look on his face, head held high. Brett was ready to take on the world, or at least the river that would be their home for the next few days.

3

Ellie stood in the parking lot of WANC with the other cadets, waiting for their promised transportation. Her stomach was in knots, but she'd spent all night reading up on the plants native to the region that could be used for food or medicine as a way to soothe her nerves. As she packed her backpack the night before, she tried not to worry about the skills of her partner. If needed, she knew she had enough knowledge and abilities to get them both out of the wilderness safely—and on time to meet their deadline. Ellie did not need luck to ace this assessment. She was skilled and educated on the outdoors, and water be damned; she would do great.

She scanned the sea of classmates for her partner.

"Hey," a warm voice said behind her. Ellie jumped as the words wiggled down her ear canal, sending tantalizing shockwaves down her spine. Somehow,

Brett's voice so close excited her body, causing her to long for closeness like a bee drawn to the pollen of a beautiful flower, opening wide for it to consume.

"Hey," she repeated, spinning around to face him while processing this new feeling he drew out of her. The sensation was strange. One that Ellie had not felt for some time. It definitely was not a post-experimentation thing that had happened in her new shifter life, and her limited memories of the time before left her unable to recall any past romantic partners.

Ellie swallowed her thoughts to keep her focus, though it was hard when she caught sight of the muscles she didn't know Brett had, which were straining against his long-sleeved shirt, filling it out in all the right ways. It was far different from the bulky sweaters he usually wore.

"New shirt?" she asked, watching the morning sun shimmer in the short waves of his brown hair, bringing out copper undertones.

A slow, wide grin spread across his face. "Yeah," he replied, his voice soft as he looked to the ground. "I thought I would need some moisture-wicking materials for our adventure."

"You did?"

"Of course." He patted his backpack. "Went to the old sporting goods store and loaded up."

She couldn't help the tingle of excitement that ran through her with the news that Brett really was taking the assignment seriously—he wanted a good grade too! She was beyond pleased to see how much preparation Brett had put into this assignment. Now she just had to get beyond the fact that a thin section of rubber would be keeping her out of the water, and she'd be just peachy.

Grayson began rattling off commands from the front of their group, separating them out depending on where and how they were to be transported to their assignment. Ellie and Brett were to be bussed to a section of the river where they would be supplied a raft.

"Are you ready?" Brett asked as he moved his weight from one foot to the other while they waited to board their transportation.

Ellie nodded as she picked up her pack. "Let's go on an adventure!" They were really doing it, really going outside on a trip away from WANC, the library, and her computer. True, she exercised outdoors on campus, but she always felt tethered to the Academy. This would be the perfect opportunity to allow herself the mental freedom of forgetting this was an assignment.

The morning sun warmed her skin as she followed Brett onto the bus. It was going to be a hot day. Actually, a hot weekend if the weather report was to be trusted. She tried to pretend she hadn't also read that there was a chance of thunder-storms throughout the weekend. The idea threatened to ruin Ellie's good mood and hopes for the trip since rain increased the chances of flash flooding—and increased her risk of getting soaked. The cat inside her shook at the thought, but she pushed past it. She would have to get used to the idea that getting wet was inevitable. If she was on a mission as a FUC agent, she would not have time to worry about preventing damp feet if things went sideways. It was a fact she—and the cat inside her— would have to learn to accept. It was something she felt she never dealt with when she was human. Ellie would have to work on channeling her happy memories of water to help get her cat-side past its fears—or at least remind herself of the videos that Brett had shown her. Cats *could* enjoy the water. She doubted she was one of them, but at least it wasn't the worst thing that could happen if she did get wet.

Silently, she filed onto the bus with Brett, behind the other cadets who would be dropped off before them.

"Are you okay?" Brett asked as they sat down, his voice gentle and caring. She looked at him, seeing his hazel eyes softened in worry for her.

How did his calmness send such a wave of comfort to her? Did sloths have some kind of super-power to do that?

"What?" She hoped she didn't look like she was losing it. It took every fiber of her being to resist the urge to gnaw on her fingernails, but she hadn't realized she was fidgeting with the hem of her shirt.

"You seem nervous," Brett explained with his brows knitted together in worry as he regarded her face.

Ellie shook her head, brushing it off, not wanting her partner to needlessly worry about her well-being. "I was just giving myself a pep talk." She hoped *that* didn't sound too weird.

Brett chuckled. "I did the same thing last night." His words instantly put Ellie at ease. Just knowing that Brett had insecurities reminded her that almost everyone struggled with self-confidence. It was also great to learn that others had conversations with themselves on a regular basis.

"How do you handle taking showers?" Brett asked as the bus headed away from campus. The moment he asked it, he pictured Ellie in the scenario—naked body and all! Quickly, he clarified his reason for asking. "I mean because you don't like water. Um. Your cat, does it not like showers?"

Adding in the word *cat* didn't help him remove the image from his mind. He frantically tried to think of anything other than what lay between Ellie's legs. *Baseball. Architecture. Complex math equations.*

Ellie, luckily, seemed to have no idea what a

struggle Brett had put himself into. She chuckled before answering his question. "That's different." The dark shadows danced off of her shoulders as she shrugged them.

"How is that different?" Brett wondered aloud. He hoped that if he could talk it out with Ellie, she would be less apprehensive on their trip. Brett knew that his ability to help her focus on the task at hand—and not the water below them—would be paramount to them completing the assignment and getting a good grade.

"The water's warm, for one thing." She pursed her lips in thought, cocking her head to the side for a moment. Her brows wrinkled as she squinted, as if trying to see the answer before her. "I don't shower with my clothes on, for starters, but in all serious-ness, I think it's because I can control it. I start the water when I am ready and end it when I am done."

Brett rubbed his chin, trying to figure out how Ellie could use that kind of thinking to her advantage on their journey. Since Brett excelled at computers, it helped him to view people like living systems. Every program was quirky, and he had to figure out how to use its language to get it to complete tasks. People were similar. They viewed the world through their experiences, their own words, and their meaning. If he could help Ellie to shift her perspective, he could get her to see the river wasn't so different from taking a shower. It all involved water.

"Did you choose to take this class?" he asked, hoping the answer was yes.

She lifted a blonde brow in curiosity. "I did. Why?"

"Did you know that an outdoors survival assignment was part of it?"

"Yes." Her answer was nervous, unsure of where the conversation was going.

"Think of that like mentally turning on the water. In a way, you choose this. Maybe you didn't pick the location, but you knew you would be outdoors. It rains outside. That can't be controlled. But you could have decided on a class that didn't have a wilderness survival project. Yet still, you *chose* this one." Brett did his best to keep his voice soft so he didn't sound like he was lecturing her. He just hoped he was going about the situation in the right way. He didn't want to offend Ellie. He just wanted to help her. To put her at ease.

A distant look washed over Ellie's face as if she were miles away. She bit the edge of her lip. The action lit a fire in Brett's soul, sending shivers down his spine. He wanted to know what it would feel like if her teeth nibbled on parts of his body. He pushed the thought down. He needed to focus.

"I guess you are right. If I think of it that way, this feels less... scary." Her shoulders rounded as she relaxed, leaning back into the seat of the bus. The tension in her body deflated with a long sigh. Her rigid shadows softened into slow-moving arcs, rolling off her arms.

Brett nodded. "Acceptance is huge. And it's accomplished by a small change in perception." He smiled triumphantly, hoping the hardest part of the trip was over. If Ellie could relax, then she could focus. Which would help him to concentrate on the task at hand.

Ellie smiled brightly. "Thank you."

Her words warmed Brett's heart.

The bus was like a beacon as the sun's rays reflected off of it. Dr. Smith watched it pull out of FUCN'A. The brush shrouded him and his binoculars as he watched the shadow cat step onto the vehicle, her dark matter flowing off of her in swirling waves.

Interesting.

The girl was far more valuable to his next set of experiments than he had originally realized.

Dr. Smith slowly pulled the receiver out of his pocket, careful not to disturb the greenery around him, as he didn't need to attract any unwanted attention. With the press of a button, he activated the tracking device he'd had his minion hide in her backpack when it was still in her room. He needed to catch that kitty, and it would be much easier to do that when she was far away from WANC, the FUC agents, instructors, and other cadets.

When Dr. Smith's minion reported on the assignment the girl would be on, Dr. Smith couldn't believe his ears. They were practically gift-wrapping the shifter for him.

The round red glow on the display of the device in his hand indicated that the tracker was working. While Dr. Smith's minion could not provide most of the details of the assignment the cadets were on, Dr. Smith knew they would be left unattended—unprotected!—in the wilderness. It provided him with the perfect opportunity to pluck the kitten from the safety of her new nest. Then she would be his to control.

As the bus pulled out of the facility, the blinking red light on his display moved to show its location on the GPS. Now all he had to do was follow from a safe distance and claim his prize. He smiled wickedly at the thought. Science was his mistress, and the thought of a girl who could bend light around her like a cocoon was orgasmic.

$$4$$

Brett and Ellie were the last cadets left on the bus waiting for their drop-off point. The rest had been dropped off at various locations around the woods and on the river.

They'd reviewed their supplies—each team of cadets was given pouches of food—and, as they'd already decided, they split up their rations so they would each carry half. They couldn't hunt or fish, since there was no way to tell if creatures they encountered in the wild were natural animals or were actually shifters—due to the park not being certified hunting land—so the rations were to ensure no mistake was made and the cadets didn't starve on their journeys.

Brett wondered if Grayson gave some of his classes assignments in certified land, where shifting was prohibited. In those areas, no shifters were allowed to be in animal form. Otherwise, they would risk being killed by others who enjoyed hunting as a pastime—in season, of course. While as a sloth, Brett wasn't exactly a target during open season, he much preferred the challenge of needing to ration their food to getting into a situation where he *needed* to shift, but that meant facing the possibility of being mistaken for something that *was* being hunted.

Brett carefully folded up the map he had been studying. "Here," he said, offering the plastic-coated chart to her.

Ellie gave him a curious glance, raising one eyebrow before plucking the map from his fingers and cramming it into her sack.

"I was going to make us a copy, but when I was in the library, Albert was helping me on the big photocopy machine, and he pointed out that a non-laminated version wasn't going to last for long out there. So, instead, I just memorized it." That, and the laminated surface kept reflecting in places whenever they tried to copy it, and though Brett had been determined, eventually the owl shifter had decided he'd wasted enough paper and nearly kicked Brett out of the library.

Ellie cut him off. "We are *not* going to get separated."

He smiled and shook his head. "I think nature does what it wants."

"All right, cadets," Grayson shouted from the front

of the bus, the urgency in his voice making Ellie jump. "Grab your gear. We are at your drop-off point." He hopped off the bus before them—just as he'd done with each other group—and waited impatiently for them to follow him.

Ellie stood, grabbing her backpack without a second thought. It weighed heavily in her arm but felt more bearable after she slung it over her shoulder. Brett had urged her to carry the tent, saying that if they were separated, she would be miserable without it—especially if it rained.

When she'd attempted to protest, Brett explained that he would be content sleeping in a tree in his sloth form. The feeling of someone looking out for her was foreign and uncomfortable for some reason. She racked through the volumes of memories, neatly categorized in her books, but found nothing useful that could explain. She would just have to get used to Brett's chivalry.

Ellie squinted in the hot sun as she stepped off of the bus, grunting slightly as she adjusted to the weight of her pack. She couldn't argue with Brett's logic, though. He was right. If she had to sleep without a tent and it was raining, she would be beyond miserable. The thought alone threatened to allow anxiety to take hold of her, but she pushed it down, focusing on the lush natural world that opened up before her.

Grayson had charged ahead across the white,

rocky, and uneven shore. Ellie took her time choosing her footing, careful to select the stones that felt sturdy and wouldn't twist under her weight. Brett was not as surefooted. She paused when she heard rumbling behind her, and she watched his arms stretch out as he struggled to keep his balance as the rocks shifted and rolled under his boots.

"Tap the ground and then place your foot if it feels sturdy," Ellie instructed with a patience that even she was proud of. She pushed at a rock with her toes; when it shifted, she chose another spot that didn't move to place her weight.

"They never taught that trick in class," Brett exclaimed, trying it out and beaming when it worked. His smile shone brighter than the sun. Ellie found it was infectious, and her heart sang since Brett hadn't become upset with her for explaining how to walk. He appeared to be soaking it all in and enjoying every second of it. He even threw his head back and laughed when he almost fell after choosing the wrong rock.

"You learn it with experience," Ellie explained, remembering a brief snapshot of herself as a child walking along a creek bed on wobbling, algae-covered rocks. Wherever she was and who she was with remained a blur in that memory. She had been working on coming to terms that the gaps might never be filled in. A deep sadness tugged at her. She sighed it out as they approached their raft. Sadness would have to take a number. Ellie had a course to ace.

Brett never imagined that walking on the large stones that framed the river would be more difficult than trudging across a frozen pond in dress shoes, but it somehow was. Every step threatened to twist his ankle until Ellie had offered him some lifesaving advice.

Now he put partial weight down to see if the rock would shift before taking a full step. Brett just hoped that he would be able to do more than his part on this project. He didn't want to hinder Ellie's progress. He was relieved when she joined in his laughter as he nearly tumbled over.

The large, inflated raft perched at the edge of the smooth, greyish water. Grayson stood next to it, ready to give his last bit of instruction. "Do you both know where your extraction point is?" he asked, his brow stern. Grayson hardly cracked a smile the entire time Brett knew him as his instructor. Brett imagined there wasn't much time to joke when you taught a class about survival and life-or-death situations.

"Yes," Brett stated as Ellie nodded her head, staring at the glassy waters that flowed quickly before them.

Beautiful yet dangerous.

"Good," Grayson said, picking up a wooden paddle. "This water may be smooth here, but it's fast. And there's an undertow." He looked back at them, stone-faced. "What do you do if you fall out?" he quipped.

Ellie turned slowly toward him, face pale. With a soft voice, she said, "Keep your feet up and lean back. Let your life jacket do its job." She shuddered, clearly thinking about how unpleasant it would be to her.

"Right." The corners of Grayson's mouth threatened to turn up in a smile and break his frigid expression. Was he enjoying the cadets' fear? "It will prevent you from getting stuck under debris and drowning. Wear your lifejackets and helmets at all times when in the raft"—Grayson pointed to them—"and if there are no questions, I will leave you to it."

They both shook their heads in response to his question and then thanked their instructor before Grayson marched off, gliding over the uneven stones as if they were no obstacle to him. Brett widened his eyes in amazement. He could only dream about being so surefooted in his lifetime.

Nervousness bubbled up in Brett's stomach. He wondered if he was ready for this test. This felt like a first mission, where he was on his own. But he wasn't alone. Ellie was at his side, ready for anything. Aside from wet feet. She had made that abundantly clear.

The bus revved its engine, and Brett heard it

crawl along the dirt road, leaving them completely alone. Soon, all he could hear was the lapping of the water on the rocks, and the realness of their assignment set in. Could he really do this?

One thing that put Brett's mind at ease was knowing that his sloth had innate survival skills that he could listen to when he felt stuck. Then, there was Ellie. If she was anywhere near as comfortable in the wilderness as she'd been walking over the rocks on the shore, then he believed he could count on her.

"Shall we?" he asked, keeping his voice confident and bright while stuffing down all his uncertainties. Brett knew that, aside from skill, a good attitude was essential, and he was determined to at least do that part of the assignment right.

Ellie nodded, removing her backpack and picking up the lifejacket that was waiting for her in the raft. Brett mirrored her, putting his pack back on when the lifejacket was secured.

Brett moved toward the raft and turned to her. Ellie's eyes squinted with determination as she took in the flowing river before them. She put her small hands on the rubbery edge of the raft and turned to Brett. "Let's do this before I change my mind," she spat out.

The words were out of Ellie's mouth before she could debate with herself. Ready or not, she was ready. But that was what she guessed was the best course of action. Just like ripping off a bandage. If she put in too much thought, she would be stuck, frozen forever on the bank. But if she just reacted, she would be fine. She wouldn't let herself think too much about the possibility of wet paws.

Brett's hands were soon nearing hers on the edge of the raft. Her hands sank in slightly against the air of it as she pushed it into the water. The raft bobbed as if nodding that it was ready to go.

"Get in, and I will push it out farther if I have to." Brett's words were calm and even, an anchor for Ellie to forget that all that separated her from being soaked was a thin layer of rubber.

She hopped in before sitting down, perching carefully on the swollen pontoon that bordered the watercraft. Ellie was sure to hook one of her feet under an inflated tube that ran across the boat. She reached for the paddle as Brett gave one final shove and hopped in. The raft lurched forward in an awkward bob. She gripped the smooth wood beneath her fingers as she sank the flat edge into the river. Ripples formed around its edge.

The boat surged forward as it was swept up by the strong current. Ellie felt the bottom of the raft shape itself to the river's surface. If there was a slight bump from the rock below, she could feel the shift in the raft below her. The water cooled the rubber around her, and she could feet its icy fingers through the bottom of the craft on her knee as she pressed it into the raft to keep her balance. Brett mirrored her movements on the opposite side.

Her paddle kissed the surface of the water, swirling it behind her as she paddled.

"We want to try to stay to the right. There are smaller rapids on that side up ahead." Brett pointed to the bend in the river that hid the change in water conditions.

He really has memorized the map, she thought. *Impressive.*

Then, Ellie could hear it. The faraway churning water. Like static on the radio.

The river yawned before them, and as they wound through the bend, it was a roar of white water flowing over rocks and stuck trees. Just as Brett had said, the teeth of white water appeared subdued on the right side. The left side threatened to suck them in. It foamed like a rabid animal. Brett switched the side he was paddling on to help Ellie keep them out of the raging current to their left. She watched his shoulder and back muscles tense as he dug his paddle into the rough water, urging the raft to stay out of the nasty section of the river that threatened to swallow them.

And it worked.

The nose of their boat edged toward the right side

of a large boulder, spinning them around to the slower side of the river. Some water droplets hit Ellie as the craft sloshed along, floating along the white edge of large rocks, smoothed from the wear of the flowing water. She found she didn't mind the wetness on her face. In fact, it was refreshing after all the paddling.

Soon the whitecaps dissipated, and the river was once more a smooth mirror. "What's next?" she asked Brett, wondering if all the rapids would be as manageable as the last. Ellie was ready to take on this river!

With careful movements, Brett switched back to his side of the raft. He dabbed at the sweat beading on his forehead with his long sleeve. "I think we have about a half-mile or so before we have to keep to the center." Ellie's heart swelled as he looked up at her with his hazel eyes. She pushed the feeling down. She was here to ace her class, not ogle Brett's rippled muscles in his tight shirt. But she couldn't help it. Every movement was mesmerizing to watch. Each time Brett dug the paddle into the surface of the water...

"Hey, don't stop paddling!" he cried out. "We keep going crooked!"

Ellie was pulled out of her daydream. "I didn't!" She hissed back the lie, quickly dipping the wooden edge of her paddle into the surface of the water before she was caught. So maybe her moment of distraction had put them on a crash course for the edge of rocks, which would have led to her in the exact circumstance she wanted to avoid—being *in* the river.

Get it together, Ellie, she scolded herself while Brett dragged his paddle on his side of the boat to help even them out. Soon the nose of the raft pushed back over to the middle of the river.

When Brett peered over his shoulder to make sure Ellie was paddling, she stuck her tongue out in a playful gesture. The broad blade of her paddle nipped at the water on her next stroke, and Brett chuckled, seemingly satisfied to see her hard at work.

The rock cliffs grew taller on either side of them as the river wound its way through the mountainside. The next set of rapids was a real test for them. It took all Brett and Ellie had in them to weave through the large boulders and frothy waters. Now they sat slumped in their seats, panting.

"I need a break." Brett hated to admit it, but he was running on empty. A dull ache grew in his upper back and shoulders. The sting of a growing blister could be felt brewing in the stretch of skin between his thumb and forefinger.

"Me too," Ellie huffed, eying the tall ledges around them. "Is there a place we can pull over? I can't see anything other than water." The river jutted out from the surrounding cliffs, a massive tongue in the mouth of rock, threatening to swallow them.

"Pull the map out for a second—please," Brett added, remembering his manners. The river of sweat between his shoulder blades itched, and his brain ached. "I think there's a good break point up ahead past the next set of rapids, but my mind's a little foggy right now."

Ellie unzipped the top of her backpack and pulled out the laminated map. She unfolded it in her lap and traced her finger down the blue path that represented their river. A thin sliver of shadows flowed off of her moving finger. She mouthed numbers silently, moving her lips as she counted the number of rapids they'd passed on their journey.

"Yeah," she said after a moment. "We have to stay left then veer right at this next set of rapids. Then there's a low ledge to the right that we can break, but"—she looked up at Brett, her eyes weary—"this part coming up looks rough."

Brett peered over at her lap to where her finger rested on the map. A long set of rapids awaited them. "We can do this," he finally said, swallowing hard but keeping his voice firm, confident. "It will be tough getting there, but it will be a well-earned break."

Ellie nodded, stuffing the map back into her sack before zipping it up and slinging it back over her shoulders.

Soon enough, they turned into the next bend in the river to be greeted by the roar of the rapids. The water up ahead was angry. "Focus, Ellie. We can do this!"

They dug into the water hard, pushing through the turbulent water, fighting against the river's desire to toss them toward the shore, straight into the jagged rocks.

His concentration was broken by a strange sound behind him, like a flap of enormous wings. His animal instinct screamed at him to turn around, fighting against his cadet discipline that insisted he not take his gaze off the rapids.

The boat bumped and rocked, and when they hit an especially rough rapid, Ellie screamed.

He looked over quickly to see if she'd fallen out of the boat, but to his shock, it wasn't the water swallowing her up.

It was a bird flying her away.

A giant red-tailed hawk had swooped down and plucked Ellie from the watercraft, digging its talons into the sack on her back. With a screech, it flapped its massive wings, escorting her into the sky above. They disappeared over the ledge of stone above.

"Ellie!" Brett screamed, unable to do anything to help her as the rapids sucked him in. What were the odds of this happening right at this moment? Miniscule. No, this hadn't been a coincidence. This was more like someone had planned to kidnap Ellie the second Brett would be stuck navigating the choppy water.

He backpaddled hard, steering the raft away from the sharp rocks on the water's edge. Bubbling white water threatened to tear Brett from the raft. He paddled vigorously, trying to focus his mind on the path Ellie had reviewed with him. *Stay left. Veer right,* her voice echoed in his mind.

Brett let the rapids pull him to the left. He focused downstream where the lacy white water foamed before him. Just as Ellie had said, to the right of a large boulder peering out of the river, the water wasn't as rough. He switched his grip on the paddle, digging it into the left side of the raft. This would have been difficult to manage with Ellie, but now he was alone and tired. His shoulders ached. The bursting blister burned as the skin ripped open. He ignored it, digging his paddle in harder, pushing the raft to the right, to calmer waters.

Just as he hoped, the water sucked him over. The raft bobbed over submerged rocks, flowing through the white water. A spray of water splashed in his face as he narrowly missed running over a tree stump. The bottom of the raft bubbled beneath him as he flowed over the rough waters.

The gravelly rocks at the side of the river were a welcoming sight ahead. It was right where Ellie had said it would be. Digging his paddle into the water, he pushed with all his might. Pain from the blister on his thumb bit into him as the wooden shaft continued to agitate his skin. Brett barely noticed. All he cared about was that the nose of the raft pointed to the shore. He paddled until the tip of the craft slid over the rocky shore. Quickly, Brett hopped out, using his remaining strength to pull the boat onto the shore.

He collapsed onto his back, not caring how the stones dug into his sore muscles. The white of the blinding sun cut into his skin with a searing heat. Brett covered his eyes with his arm, not sure what to do next. Ellie was gone.

When he finally found the strength, he sat up, peering into the treetops where Ellie had vanished across the river, wondering if he should wait for her to find him or brave the wilderness to find her.

5

———

Ellie didn't know what hit her—or, more correctly, what had snatched her off the raft. At first, she thought a bump in the river had knocked her off. Fear gripped her as she anticipated the icy fingers of the water pulling her under. But that never happened.

Ellie opened her eyes to see the craft shrink beneath her as she gained altitude. The straps of her backpack bit into her armpits. Her mind began to make sense of the situation. Something had her by the backpack, and it was pulling her upwards, away from the river. Away from Brett.

Ellie silently thanked Paige for the hours they spent together, practicing various forms of shifting. Ellie, being a former human, did not have the experience that Paige had, being born a shifter. Paige patiently walked her through shifting just her eyes or just her hands. Ellie never knew how useful it could be until this very moment.

She focused on her nails, urging them to grow into long, sharp kitty claws. The bones popped in her fingers as they began shrinking up into giant paws. Ellie fought the urge to dig her needle-like nails into the beast that held her, knowing she would have to control her fall. If she dropped from the sky in the wrong area, she would surely plummet to her death. No one wanted that. Especially Ellie.

The edge of the river disappeared into a canopy of green, and Ellie grew aware of a large pine nearing them, its bough reaching out to her. She took that as a sign.

Ellie reached up with her cat claws and embedded them into the tough scales of the beast holding her. One talon released her as the beast screeched above her. Without hesitation, she sank her claws into the creature once more. Its blood dripped onto her face, but it refused to let go.

The tree was beneath her now. She stretched as far as her arms would allow and raked her nails down the leg of the bird. Finally, it could hold her no longer.

Ellie fell from its clutches, helpless to gravity. The scratchy needles of the pine tree clawed along her skin as she fell, bouncing from one bough to the next. The branches became larger the farther down she fell, slowing her descent. She used her claws to stop herself, hugging the tree, grabbing for anything that could stop her.

Knowing she was not out of danger yet, she willed the light to bend around her, enveloping both her and her backpack. She felt the shadows wrap around her as she became one with the tree to anyone looking.

Ellie hoped the sap and needles that clung to her from her fall would be enough to mask her scent as well. It was still new to her how strong the sense of smell was to shifters. It took a lot of getting used to, and she didn't always remember how strong her scent was to others. It was not a mistake she could afford to make now.

The giant hawk circled overhead, screeching, the sound piercing her eardrums. She tried not to wince at the sound, afraid any movement in the tree would give away her position. The cries of the bird softened as it scanned the forest farther away, but still, Ellie refused to move, afraid it could see her.

She hugged her body tightly to the tree until the cries of the bird of prey vanished, and the normal sounds of the forest returned. Chipmunks chittered below on the ground as a smaller bird chirped around her, as if they wanted to tell her the coast was clear.

Ellie felt a sigh of relief escape her lips. Her shoulders shuddered, tired from paddling and then from hanging in the air by her backpack. She hoped she had enough energy to make it to the ground—it would suck to end up being the cliché of a cat stuck in a tree. The shadows around her shimmered, signaling that her energy was running low. Soon she wouldn't be able to remain invisible, but, for now, she willed the shadows to keep her hidden, hoping she could hold out a bit longer.

Ellie let her fingers lengthen to human hands, yet allowed the claws to remain. Slowly, she made her descent, careful that each branch could carry her weight before she stepped fully on it. She kept her hands and feet close to the trunk of the tree, where the branches were stronger. Sap and pine needles stuck to her claws and fingers, and she tried not to think about how long it would take to wash off.

Little by little, she made progress down the tree until her boots touched the soft ground of the forest floor.

Only then did she let the shadows go, allowing herself to become visible once more. She braced herself, waiting for a creature to pop out and grab her, as if something had been waiting for her to show herself once more.

Nothing happened.

She relaxed, letting the claws recede and flatten back into human nails. Her fingertips tingled in the process, a sensation Ellie still wasn't used to, and she clenched and released her fingers to try to make it stop. Eventually, the discomfort went away.

She peered up, trying to see through the thick branches to the sky above. She could hardly make out the blue of the sky through the canopy of green. There would be no way she could spot that bird from here.

She hoped the reverse was true as well.

Ellie plopped down on the carpet of red needles and brown leaves at her feet. They crunched beneath her. She unzipped her bag, pulling out her compass and map. She didn't think that the fall had left her concussed, but she did still feel a bit disoriented. Her breath came in fast waves, mingling with her racing heart.

She slowed her breathing, straining to hear the sounds of the river. If she was correct with her positioning, she shouldn't be too far from it—and Brett. She hoped he waited on the shore where they planned a break. Otherwise, she didn't know how she would find him.

What if something happened to him? What if a giant bird plucked him from the raft as well? Or what if he couldn't control the raft on his own and he crashed into the rocks? Ellie couldn't bear the thought. They could both be lost forever.

She forced herself to push those thoughts from her mind.

After standing up and slinging her pack over her shoulder, she set out toward what she hoped was the river. The path wasn't clear, and she had to weave around brush and carefully step over broken logs and stumps.

Her cat would have an easier time walking it, but she couldn't shift if she wanted to keep her pack, which contained all her food and supplies for the journey. There was no way her tiny cat-self could carry the pack or even drag it. She would just have to bound through the branches and brambles the best she could in her human form.

The white noise of the river beyond grew louder, coming in over the next edge of rock before her. She toed the cliff, peering at the rapids and white water below. Squinting from the sun reflecting off the water, she peered downriver at a grey shoreline opposite her. A black, oval object rested on it. *Our raft!*

She strained her ears for the sound of feathers and flapping but could hear nothing over the roar of the water below. After not seeing anything in the sky above, Ellie screamed out, "Brett!" while waving her arms and being careful to not lose her balance and tumble into the raging water below.

The smooth stones of the shoreline did not make the most restful place, but Brett was exhausted. His mind swam with scenarios about the bird who took Ellie. He knew she came to FUC academy as a rescued and rehabilitated experiment. What if the scientist who created her wanted her back? Ellie's abilities were amazing—even by shifter standards—so what if an evil person wanted her for their own gain?

The thought made Brett know that he had to try to find her. He propped up on his elbows, staring at the white, frothy water. If Brett could even make it across the fast-moving river, he wasn't sure if he could climb the sheer cliff that towered on the opposite side. It did not appear easy for Brett to climb. None of it would be an easy task.

That was when Brett spotted movement.

Suddenly appearing at the top of the ledge as if borne from the forest shimmering behind her was Ellie. She waved her arms frantically. Her pink lips moved as if she were yelling, but Brett couldn't make out the sounds. He popped up off the stones and swayed his arms above his head to show Ellie he saw her.

Now he just had to figure out how to get across the raging, unforgiving river and climb up the sheer rock at the other side. He swallowed hard, taking in the obstacle before him. He would need a miracle, or a good plan, at least.

Brett scanned the opposite shoreline, watching the angry river turn smooth as glass. The rock was broken up in chucks and jagged ledges, and an uprooted tree cascaded down into the water, giving Brett the perfect place to tie the raft and climb up.

He waved his arms back at Ellie, catching her attention, and pointed downriver to signal where he intended to cross to pick her up. She nodded in large movements before running off, disappearing back into the sea of greenery behind her.

Brett scanned the blue sky for any large predatory birds. Nothing dotted the scenery above aside from a few wispy clouds in the distance. Brett hoped that his sore muscles were rested enough when he pushed the raft back into the water. The craft bobbed as he hopped in, instantly reaching for his paddle. He dipped the wood into the river with vigor, throwing water behind him with each push. The small rubber boat surged forward toward the opposite shore, but it was difficult for Brett to stop it from being sucked into the set of rapids around the next bend. He strained against the current, pushing hard with the paddle. His muscles screamed in protest.

The rocky shoreline came closer with each stroke. The tree's bare branches reached into the water, and tiny ripples surrounded the twigs that breached its surface. Brett reached out, grabbing a dead arm of the tree. He pulled the raft into the edge of rock and carefully tied a rope to anchor the raft to it.

"I'm coming down!" Ellie cried from above, her voice shaky.

Brett peered up at her as she eyed the path of jagged rock and the broken tree that led to the river below. "Throw me your backpack," Brett called up, hoping the trek down would be easier on Ellie without the extra weight.

She hesitated as his words sank in, toeing the edge of the cliff twenty feet above him. Her blue eyes met Brett's, and finally, she shrugged out of the straps of her sack before dropping it toward him. It bounced off a rock ledge halfway down, sending a small cascade of pebbles and dirt into the raft. Brett closed his eyes, coughing and sputtering as the debris hit his face. Then her pack hit him in the chest, and he nearly fell backward from the force.

Somehow, he stayed upright. The bobbing craft threatened to knock him down as it shifted under him from his own movements and the flowing water beneath him.

"Sorry!" Ellie called down, wincing at the sight.

"It's okay," Brett called up, wiping at his eyes while trying to keep his balance in the raft. His vision blurred as tears welled up to clean out the dust. His legs wobbled under his weight as the raft jostled in the current from the force of the backpack falling into it.

"Sit down before you fall overboard," Ellie commanded from above, her voice stern. Brett did as she directed, watching her maneuver down the rock and tree, using the branches as a ladder. The water was a cold kiss through the rubbery bottom of the craft as Brett observed her, helpless to assist.

The raft nodded as Ellie carefully stepped down

from the tree above. Brett noticed the black sap that clung to her hands as she tried to brush them off on her pants. "What happened?" he inquired as she sat down next to him, her shadows jolting off of her arms in agitated waves as she shook. Brett handed her a canteen as she panted, catching her breath and wiping at the sweat beading on her brow.

Ellie's throat bobbed as she greedily chugged the water Brett had offered her. The cool liquid slid down her throat, quenching her thirst.

Since when does a bird catch a cat? Shouldn't it be the other way around? The tired thought popped out of her weary mind. Ellie was pissed that the drama of being kidnapped had ruined the breaktime she was looking forward to. And it left her with more questions than answers.

"I really don't know," she admitted to Brett after getting her fill of water. "A giant hawk or something plucked me out of the raft. I was able to shift my hands into claws and scratch the shit out of it until it let me go." She peered up the cliff, noting the green canopy of the forest trees above. Ellie realized how lucky she was to have slid down the pine tree like she did. She could have very easily been injured from the fall. "I caught one of the pine trees on the way down and hid until I couldn't hear the bird anymore."

Brett's hazel eyes were wide as she recounted what happened. "I am so glad you are okay." The words were soft, barely audible over the trickling of the water around them.

She sighed deeply, glad that the cliff above them should be hiding them slightly from any creatures in the sky that might approach. "I just want to eat." She rubbed her stomach as it growled. Ellie hadn't realized how hungry she was. She'd been too busy fighting a giant bird and trying not to die. Good thing kitties were known to land on their feet. And by some miracle, she didn't get stuck in that tree. That would have been a kick in the ass. She smiled at the thought as she opened her backpack to look for the food rations inside.

"What's so funny?" Brett asked, pulling a silver pouch from his backpack.

"Firemen have to get cats out of trees." She ripped open the pouch labeled tuna fish. The feline inside of her purred, happy with her selection.

Brett stared at her, a blank look on his face. His mouth hung open for a second, causing Ellie to chuckle. "I don't get it," he finally said, tearing open his own silver pouch of food.

"A tree broke my fall, and I didn't get stuck in it." Laughter bubbled out of her. She swallowed her food quickly so she wouldn't choke or spit it all over her companion. Brett's brow furrowed. He looked lost, so she explained. "I'm a cat shifter. Cats in trees…"

A smile tugged at the corners of Brett's thin lips. "I don't know why that went over my head."

Ellie put a hand on his arm to reassure him. "We both had a rough half-hour. Don't beat yourself up over it." She beamed a smile at it. The one that put people at ease.

It worked. Brett leaned back into the inflated tube on the side of the raft behind him, pushing his meal up out of the pouch. He swallowed, eying the sky with a nervous look on his face. "How do we keep you hidden from that thing when we go back out on the open water?"

The thought gnawed at Ellie as well. The cliffs sheltered them a bit, but she was basically a sitting duck out in the raft. If that hawk found her once, it could again. *Who was behind it?* She remembered the scientist and shifter who were after her friend Paige last year. As far as she knew, they were all apprehended. But someone out there wanted her, probably for her unique abilities. "We could always stash the raft and try to hike the forest along the river," she mused aloud.

Brett chewed his food, squinting as he thought about her plan. "We could do it, but it will be much longer, and we'll risk not making it to the pickup location in time."

Ellie split open her pouch and licked up the tuna that remained, her stomach churning and hungry for more. She didn't care how odd she looked. The miles ahead would be treacherous, and she was ravenous.

"I'd rather fail this class than be kidnapped and experimented on again." She hoped Brett wasn't taken aback by her bluntness. He nodded as if this were the most normal conversation in the world.

"That's a good point." Brett sucked the remaining food out of his pouch and rubbed his chin, seemingly deep in thought. After some consideration, he added, "And I am sure Grayson will understand we had extraneous circumstances surrounding our lateness to the rendezvous point."

Ellie felt a pang of guilt. She went into this trip thinking Brett would be the one to ruin her chances of a good grade. Now it seemed she was the one to derail the assignment. "I am sorry if I am the reason you don't pass this project."

Brett smiled, showing a row of perfect teeth and somehow convincing Ellie that everything would be okay. "I don't care about that now. All I care about is that I get you back safely, by any means necessary."

Ellie returned the grin, feeling that with Brett by her side, she could take on an army of giant birds.

6

They had to make it a bit farther down before they could abandon the river in favor of the forest.

They navigated the next set of rapids, both of them taking turns to watch the sky above while the other paddled. Ellie had pointed out after studying the map that their extraction point was on the opposite shore, so they had no choice but to fight through the rough patch of water before they had another low section of stone where they could dock. Brett didn't like the idea of leaving Ellie so exposed but didn't see they had much of a choice.

His heart thumped in his ears with anxiety as she struggled to watch the skies above while navigating the white, frothy water. That was when he saw it. A log submerged in the water before them. The raft was headed straight for it.

"Backpaddle!" he cried, but it was too late. The

craft hit the log with such force he was launched from it.

Cold water ran its icy fingers along his skin. The roaring of the river above was silenced as his head dipped below the surface from the force of his impact. His backpack threatened to pull him under, but the lifejacket that hugged his body went to work. After what felt like minutes underwater, Brett surfaced to hear screams. It was Ellie.

He sputtered after taking a breath filled with bubbling water. He splashed his arms around, trying to lean back to keep his toes up out of the water as he had been instructed. "El-Ellie!" he called out after a cough.

"I'm okay!" her strained voice called from behind him. "Swim to shore after we clear the rapids!"

The water pulled Bret along. He flowed past the whitewater that broke over large boulders to his left. It was as if the water knew how to pull him along to safety. At times he fought to keep his toes up, knowing that if they fell beneath the surface of the angry water, he could easily be trapped under rocks, stumps, or debris. And if that happened, he could be done for.

Soon the water quieted. Brett doggy-paddled to shore, fighting the urge to shift. He'd have an easier time swimming but would lose all their supplies. That would make their bad day worse.

The water rippled around him and lapped on the

rocks as he pulled himself onto the shore. He turned to the river, frantic to find Ellie's location. Her pale face shone, wet with water, eyes wide with fear and discomfort. "You're almost here!" He tried comforting her, urging her to shore.

Her hands clawed at the stone as she tried to pry herself from the icy grip of the river. Brett rushed to help her, pulling her up by the straps of her backpack. She collapsed in a heap on the shore. Brett let her catch her breath as he eyed the sky, wary the hawk would come back while they were at their worst. But nothing flew overhead save for a bunch of lazy fluffy clouds that temporarily doused them in shadow. He shivered at the change in temperature.

He glanced at the angry water, watching the overturned raft bob off into the distance before it disappeared into the frothy, white water of the next set of rapids. Brett let out a sputtering sigh as their means of transportation vanished. He leaned back into the rocky shore as Ellie caught her breath. The wispy clouds floated overhead. Lucky for them, it was the only thing he could see in the sky for miles.

"Are you okay?" Brett asked after rolling over on his side, facing her.

Ellie unbuckled her helmet and did her best to squeeze the water out of her short locks. It dripped its chilly fingers down her back, unleashing a shiver. Her shoulders shook, but she didn't dare move into the sun and out of the shade of the rocks and trees above for fear of being seen by that giant bird again.

The cat inside of her hissed and howled. It took every fiber of her being to not rip her clothes off. The water sliding down her skin was uncomfortable, almost unbearable. And cold. The longer she sat on the bank, her body heat seemed to seep into the water on her skin. Ellie wanted to shake it off but knew that would do no good. Plus, she had other things to worry about: like that hawk coming back to snatch her up and make bird food out of her.

"Yeah," she finally answered, making herself sound calm, though she wanted to scream. She crossed her arms over her chest, trying to keep some of the heat in. The day was warm, but the water was not. And neither was the shade when one was soaking wet. "Do you think that hawk will come back?" she asked, scanning the sky.

"I don't know." Brett scratched at his neck after removing his helmet. A small stream of water trickled down his temple. He ruffled his hair, which had begun to curl in a most attractive way. "I don't think we should take any chances. We should keep tight to the trees if we can."

They glanced back at the gravelly path that seemed to lead up to the top of the rock ledge and forest above. It was probably a water runoff, but with the day being dry so far, it should be a nice and easy way for them to get away from the river where they were now stranded. Their little shore of rock was eaten by the towering rock ten feet in either direction, and they would either have to climb up and make their way through the dense woods above or swim downriver. The latter option was not safe, which left only one way forward.

Ellie looked to the forest above, trying to take her mind off of how Brett's untamed hair left her stomach bubbling with excitement. Or the way his wet shirt clung to his sculpted muscles. She needed to focus. Not only was their assignment on the line, but their lives were too. Aside from the rogue bird that had tried to scoop her up, who knew what dangers lurked in the forest?

She stood, hating the way her sopping clothes adhered to her body. They pulled on her every time she took a step. Water continuously dripped down her back and arms as it leached from her clothes. It was cringeworthy. Her inner cat was screaming, "Get it off! Get it off!" so loudly she could hardly focus on anything else.

Well, she did have one other clear thought in her head: they'd left their raft behind and let it float away, which would likely result in a failing grade for the assignment.

She gritted her teeth, the tension mounting in her jaw, giving her a stress headache. She must have made a face because Brett said, "Let's keep going a little farther, then take a break. Might be good to shift and lay our clothes out to dry."

She nodded. The thought was enticing. She could dry off in cat form and not have to worry about damp clothes and wet feet. A smile tugged at the corners of her lips. Ellie wanted to shift now, but they *had* to keep moving. At least for a little bit more. She tried to channel those happy human memories of swimming in lakes as a child, but it didn't help. Wet garments equaled a miserable Ellie.

She smiled at Brett. "I think that's a great idea. Let's climb up this first and then work on finding a spot to camp," she blurted out before she changed her mind and tried to convince Brett to let her shift now. He'd have to carry her backpack if she did. She knew he would. But then her outfit would never dry crumpled up inside of her bag. And the thought of putting wet clothes back on was worse than wearing them currently.

The white stones of the path tumbled out from under her as she tried to make her way up the slope. She cascaded dust, dirt, and rock on poor Brett behind her. "Sorry," she said over her shoulder each time she heard him sputtering or coughing behind her. A few tiny saplings and thick patches of weeds helped her along, as she used them as a makeshift rope to haul herself up the side of the rocky slope.

She could move faster with her arms helping her climb.

As she stepped onto the flatter surface at the top, a warm feeling bubbled up inside of her. She was triumphant. No stupid bird or rock ledge was going to keep her down today. Raft or not, they were going to make it out alive—not to mention ace their assignment. Ellie bit back a cheer that threatened to burst out of her lips, and instead of raising her arms to twirl into a happy dance, she quickly ducked into the green brush and pulled the shadows around her, aware that she still needed to hide from her bird foe.

The sun danced in Brett's glistening hair as he popped onto the top of the embankment. Dust caked his face, and pale streaks remained where either water or sweat dripped a clean path down his visage. Brett wiped the remaining dirt off by pulling up the bottom of his shirt, revealing his tight abs. Ellie watched a drop of water slide down his body. It ignited a hunger inside of her. She thirsted to lick the water off of his perfect form.

"Ellie?" he asked, looking around for any sign of her in the trees. The anxiety in his strained voice brought Ellie out of her mind.

She jumped out of the brush and unwrapped the light from around her, letting herself be seen once more. "Sorry. I was hiding from any potential avian enemies."

Brett's shoulders relaxed with a sigh. "No problem. I'd become invisible, too, under the circumstances."

Ellie looked to the forest floor, tracing her eyes along a dried-up stream bed that seemed to roam in the general direction they were traveling. "I guess we should march on. Let's follow this for as long as we can," she directed, indicating the stony path that weaved around the trunks of the large trees.

Brett nodded in agreement. They trudged through the trees, dripping wet and slightly miserable. Ellie just hoped that whoever sent the bird after her didn't have a cougar or something in their arsenal to dispatch next.

7

———

Ellie felt the sting of a blister forming as her wet boots rubbed on her heel with each painful step. She loved hiking but hated wet footwear, and this was becoming torture. She had led them away from the dried-up stream bed when it weaved off too far from the river below them. Now they fought their way through vines and underbrush that seemed to enjoy slapping her in the face every chance that they got. And if one more viny bramble tugged at her legs or scratched her bare arms, she might scream.

After she powered through, a thorny bush bit at her flesh. She shouted to no one in particular, "I need a break!" With a huff, she sat on the spongy remains of a rotting stump. She almost hoped that the hawk would come back so she could take out her anger on it. She was one pissed-off pussy. Ellie wanted nothing more than to sink her claws into something to relieve the energy that was bubbling up inside her.

Brett plopped down next to her in the blanket of red pine needles and dead leaves that coated the forest floor. His chest swelled and deflated as he tried to catch his breath.

"Do you know what time it is?" she asked, trying to ignore the pain that bit into her heel as she pried her left boot off.

Brett moved his arm and glanced at the waterproof watch, peeking out from beneath his sleeve, on his wrist. "It's coming up to dinner time. Maybe we should try to make camp somewhere. It's been a day." His voice was soft, almost pleading, as if Ellie would insist on continuing.

Yes, they were now on an impossibly long hike by foot, and their grade was on the line, but they couldn't keep going without proper rest. Even Ellie realized that.

She glanced down the way they came. They had been heading up-slope for a while. No wonder they were exhausted.

She tied the shoelaces of her boots together and tossed them around her neck. "I can't put these back on," Ellie explained to Brett after watching him arc a curious eyebrow at her. "I'd rather take my chances walking barefoot than put wet footwear back on. My boots are a form of torture at this point." Her toes curled into the soft soil, thankful to be free. Only one of her blisters had ripped open, but both heels burned.

Brett nodded, then pointed toward a possible clearing in the trees. "It looks like there is an opening over there."

The sunlight filtered through the clearing, and as welcoming and warm as it appeared, Ellie felt hesitation gnaw at her. She feared the hawk would be waiting for her, ready to swoop down the second she entered the clearing. As if sensing her apprehension, Brett said with a smile, "I'll check it out first if you want to wait here. If the coast is clear, I'll call for you. You can join me in the sun, hang up your clothes, and shift into your cat."

Ellie nodded with more energy than she thought she had left. She leaned back on an elbow and watched Brett hustle up the slope, weaving through trees.

Brett scanned the skies to ensure Ellie's safety. After seeing nothing but normal-sized birds and seagulls, he called back down to her.

"Go ahead and shift," he told her once she joined him. "I'll keep my back turned so you can hang up your clothes."

She didn't object, which he was glad for. It pained him to see Ellie so miserable. She had to trek through the forest in uncomfortably wet clothes after the frightening event of being kidnapped and flown away by a bird *and* later tossed from their raft into the river. It was a major credit to her that she had been able to hold it together for that long.

While Ellie presumably shifted, Brett pulled out everything they needed to set up camp. He struggled with the tent poles, finding them not as easy to unfold and put together as he imagined, and he suddenly wished he'd thought to practice a bit before they were out there.

Then, Ellie purred, rubbing her cat body on his ankles. He looked down, seeing the silky creature, and peered back where she'd hung her clothes. They flapped in a gentle breeze on the branch of the tree overhead, basking in the light of the sun. It dropped lower in the sky as night moved in closer.

All at once, one of the tent poles sprang open in his hand, extending and catching on the nylon of the tent. As he attempted to right himself, he somehow managed to trip over Ellie.

"Sorry!" he said, wondering how much her cat instincts were a factor in if she enjoyed rubbing against him. He hoped it meant that she liked him a little bit, but couldn't be sure. His heart fluttered at the thought, but he couldn't picture a woman like her wanting anything to do with a man like him. He recalled the look she gave him in class when there were assigned to each other for this trip. The thought brewed an ache in his chest over how much his feelings were hurt.

Brett pushed the sensation away as he struggled to put the tent together. He wanted to prove to Ellie that he was an asset. That he *could* be the kind of man who could deserve someone like her.

Despite nearly being stepped on, Ellie remained close to him, bunting her head against his knee as if trying to comfort him. He sighed, bending down to scratch behind her ears. She leaned into it, purring. He hoped that she was feeling better. She had been through so much. And though getting wet had seemed to be her biggest concern before they'd set out on the adventure, it now appeared to be the least of her worries.

Brett's eyes scanned the skies once more for any creature that could snatch up the small black cat. Only regular-sized birds dotted the sky. It gave him all the more reason to get their tent set up: protection for Ellie.

After struggling to thread the tent rods through their canals, Brett—to his surprise—popped the tent up off the ground in its correct form. He smiled broadly, pleased with himself. He glanced at Ellie, curled up on the ground in a strip of sunshine. The golden sun glittered in her short black fur, and he was surprised to see that, as a cat, the usual shadows that wafted off of her when she moved were no longer there.

Brett checked her clothes hanging in the tree. He wanted something to go right for Ellie today. He flipped the garments to try to dry the other side before the sun dipped below the horizon. The day had been hot, but a low sun wasn't best for drying things. He kicked himself for not hanging his own clothing up to dry. Under his arms and the middle of his back were still damp. His pants were a different story. They didn't seem to want to dry at all.

"I'm going to get changed in the tent and try to dry my clothes for tomorrow," he said to the tiny cat. She looked at him with wide blue eyes, her pupils barely more than slits as she basked in the sunbeams. In response, she flicked the tip of her tail, and Brett assumed that meant "okay."

Brett quickly changed into his night clothes—a pair of sweatpants and a T-shirt—and exited the tent with his damp clothes balled up in his hand. He rolled up his boxers into the middle of the pile, embarrassed to have Ellie see his underwear.

He looked to the strip of sun on the ground but didn't see the black cat. Only the patted-down earth where she had previously lain remained. "Ellie?" He glanced around the opening in the forest where they had pitched their tent. His heart raced in his chest, hammering out an anxious tune. He had forgotten to check the sky before heading into the tent. What if the hawk was up there and had gotten Ellie?

Just then, a pine cone landed on his head. He

looked up to see wide blue eyes peering out of a furry black face. It was Ellie. Her claws were sunk into the bark of the soaring pine tree next to the tent. Sap clung to her long whiskers, clumping some of them together.

"Do you need help?" he asked her, unsure why she had climbed the tree to begin with.

She flicked her chin up to the sky as if searching for something that had frightened her into hiding. Brett followed suit, scanning the darkening skies above. Fluffy navy blue clouds were ushered in by a wind that was gathering its strength. Brett wondered if the thunderstorms the weather person predicted were on their way in. The possibility of rain didn't seem a strong enough reason for Ellie to be scared up into a tree, though.

That was when he saw it.

A large hawk circled into view after making a pass over the towering trees to his right. Its enormous size was enough evidence for Brett to know that this had to be a shifter. While not all shifters were larger versions of their animal form—Ellie was the size of a small housecat—the ones that dwarfed their true animal counterparts were clearly shifters.

Without warning, the foul fowl swooped down, scratching its sharp talons across Brett's forearm as he brought it up just in time to shield his face. This bird of prey was out for blood! Brett frantically searched the ground for anything he could use as a weapon. His pocketknife was zipped up in his bag inside the tent. He wouldn't go for it, though, because he didn't want to leave Ellie outside of his field of vision again.

He spotted a long and thick gnarled branch on the ground. Just as the bird screeched and swooped down for another attack, Brett picked it up and used it like a baseball bat on the creature. A crack filled the air as the bough snapped after making contact with the beast. With a shrill cry and a flutter of red-brown feathers, the animal took to the skies, disappearing once more over the sweeping green of the outstretched arms of the forest.

8

"You're bleeding." Ellie had jumped out of the tree and shifted back into human form, not caring that she now stood nude in front of Brett.

He'd saved her!

And now he was hurt.

Blood blossomed in a line down his arm where the hawk had torn at his flesh. He seemed to take no notice as it beaded before running down in a slow streak toward his fingers. Brett continued to stare at the sky where the bird had vanished as if it would appear out of thin air. Ellie gathered that could be a possibility, as she had the ability to vanish and reappear in her human form. But from what she heard at the hospital section of WANC, it seemed to be an ability not many had—if anyone else possessed it at all.

Brett glanced at his arm. "It doesn't feel that deep."

He shrugged before squinting back at the bruised sky. The sun was a red ball, dipping behind the mountains in the distance. A pastel rainbow of sunset ripped across the horizon, escorting in the inky indigo that would soon blacken to night. The wind picked up, whipping the clouds across the sky. No avian creatures could be seen.

"Let me clean you up inside the tent," Ellie proposed, reaching for her clothes, which still hung in the tree. She threw them on quickly, pleased that they were mainly dry. Her boots waited for her near the entrance of the tent. She threw them inside the door, wanting to protect them from the incoming storm—she hoped to have dry feet tomorrow.

Brett nodded before finally tearing his eyes from the sky. He gritted his teeth as he followed Ellie into the tent. "Why do you think it's after you?" he asked, referring to the hawk.

"Who knows?" Ellie snapped, sounding much harsher than she meant to. "Maybe someone farms for women off the river for their human trafficking ring."

"I'd have to assume you were one of the first victims," Brett retorted, sounding more impudent than she would have expected and once again showing her that he wasn't a pushover. "Otherwise, there would have been reports about something like that, and I'm pretty sure Grayson would have given us some kind of warning."

Ellie sighed. She supposed Brett needed to know the truth. Again, she thought about when Grayson first assigned them together, and she'd assumed Brett would be the team's dead weight. Turns out, when he admitted his handicap—that he'd never been camping before—she should have revealed hers: that she was an escaped experiment, and who knew if there were people out there looking to kidnap her back? It was right to let a partner know exactly what risks they were possibly facing.

"You're right. This area probably doesn't have an issue with hawks kidnapping random people. So, in that case, my best guess is that someone from the lab I escaped from wants me back," she explained with a shudder. She didn't like talking about the labs. It made her feel so low on the food chain. She rifled through her bag for medical supplies, pulling out the small zippered pack filled with bandages and ointment.

"I'm sorry." Brett stared at her, his expression soft with what was probably sympathy or compassion, but Ellie could only see pity.

Exactly what she hated. It didn't matter if it was from the FUC scientists or the FUCN'A staff or this quiet, sweet, undeniably appealing sloth. That look meant they were seeing her as something fragile, something less-than, something broken. But she wasn't broken, and she needed people to know that.

"I prefer to not talk about it," she snarled, automatically taking out her anxiety on Brett, though she knew she shouldn't be upset with him for just showing kindness. "Besides, who cares why I'm being targeted? It could be a hypothetical human trafficker who is a stranger to me, or it could be some unhinged scientist who is looking for me specifically. Does it matter?"

"I guess it really doesn't," Brett said, his voice soft while he looked away from her. "But I do care."

His words hit her in a strange way. She couldn't explain why knowing that Brett cared made her feel good. She ignored the sensation, focusing on the work that needed to be done.

She unzipped her little first aid kit, the buzzing of the zipper breaking the silence that had grown between them. Ellie flipped through the small single-serve packets of burn cream until she found the anti-septic salve.

"I have no idea if this will sting," she admitted after tearing off a corner of the pouch.

"It's okay. It needs to get cleaned." Brett looked back at her as she dabbed at the gash with some loose gauze from the medical pack. His eyes closed in a wince as she pressed the white cloth, soaking up the pooled blood. With caution, she squeezed some of the ointment out of the antiseptic pouch and into the wound. Brett smiled. "Doesn't hurt at all."

She felt the tension release from her body. Ellie didn't realize how nervous she was. She was so afraid to hurt Brett more than he already was. And it was all her fault. That bird was after her, not Brett.

"Are you okay?" he asked after a moment.

"I feel bad that you're injured because of me." Ellie started wrapping a bandage around the gash on his arm, careful not to make it too tight or too loose. Guilt and anxiety took turns gnawing at her stomach. "And that's on top of the fact that you're risking failing this course because of me. We're without our preferred method of transportation, so it's going to be longer to get to the extraction point, and who knows what will happen if we don't get there in time."

"I really don't think that they'll fail us." Brett put a reassuring hand on hers before he took the wrappings from her and started to pack up her kit. "They definitely won't abandon us out here forever. My guess would be that they send some agents out here to find us. That's what they're good at, you know."

He was right, at least about the last part.

"What happens if the hawk comes back before we're extracted?" she asked. "Who's to say it won't tear through our tent in the dead of night and rip you up, then snatch me up once more? You're in danger because you were assigned to be my partner. You didn't choose to be put in this position, and I don't want anything else to happen to you!"

She could feel the familiar lump of sadness form thick in her throat, threatening to choke her. Brett had done *nothing* to deserve this. Brett was the kind of guy who was *always* cheery and easygoing. He was the kind of guy that no one would say a bad thing about, who had done everything in his power to prepare for their mission, who was kind enough to let her dry off in sunbeams while he struggled to put up a fussy tent by himself for the first time.

He. Didn't. Deserve. This.

Her eyes stung as the saline of tears swelled up under her lids.

"Ellie," Brett pleaded as he regarded her face. It was apparently the magic word that opened the floodgates of emotion.

The dread that haunted her leading up to their drop-off. The anxiety of being on the river. The terror of being taken by a bird. The fear while being separated from her partner, followed by the horror of watching him get hurt in the second hawk attack. The emotions threatened to swallow her.

All of that, on top of the knowledge that she hadn't been able to escape the lab after all.

Ellie had been swallowing those feelings all day, pushing them further and further down into her gut, ignoring their very existence. She didn't have to feel them if she could pretend they weren't there. That none of it was actually happening.

It worked until her cup of emotion overflowed, and she became a blubbering mess.

She could hardly believe it was happening, that

she was sobbing like this in front of someone. That was not who she was. Ellie was the type of person who would be the captain on the bridge of a ship, steering through open waters as cool as a cucumber while the flames of the vessel surrounded her, eating at the very floor she stood on. She would sail on while the craft around her sank to the bottom of the sea. And now she was drowning.

Tears streaked down her hot face. She sniffed, not wanting Brett to see snot dripping out of her nose. She tried to talk, but the lump in her throat prevented her from doing so. Instead, she hid her face in her hands and sobbed, shoulders shuddering as if she were a volcano erupting.

Brett's warm arm wrapped around her, pressing her against his body as he hugged her into him. "It's okay." His voice was soft and gentle. It was as if he couldn't understand the precariousness of their situation. Ellie wanted to explain it all to him. She had this fear that he would think she was overreacting. She was supposed to be a future FUC agent, and she was having a difficult time mastering her emotions. It was all so much. The possible failure of their class, them probably being stranded in the Canadian wilderness forever, or him being killed while she was kidnapped.

As if her feelings were connected to Mother Nature, thunder boomed overhead, shaking the earth around them. It fueled Ellie's despair. She nestled her face into Brett's chest, wiping tears and snot onto his shirt. He wrapped his other arm around her, holding her tight. She leaned into his embrace, feeling the safety that it offered. It was a warm blanket, suffocating her fears, stifling her guilt.

Her body began to relax, loosening the tension in her muscles. Like a tidal wave, her emotions ran their course and now subsided. With a long sniff, she brought back her composure, peeling herself away from Brett to dab her face on the hem of her shirt. Exhaustion pulled at her. Her breakdown was draining.

"We're going to get through this one thing at a time," Brett finally said. "So, to make sure the hawk doesn't catch us unaware while we're sleeping, we'll take turns standing watch. In fact, you should probably get to sleep now before it's your shift." He offered her a smile, and his beautiful, magical sloth grin did its thing comforting her and making her feel like he'd sent a small flicker of joy into her dark and sad soul.

Guilt threatened to pull Ellie back under, but she thought it would be easier for Brett if she didn't argue with him. Instead, she asked, "What will you do so you don't feel alone and bored?"

Another crack of thunder roared as the drum of rain started on the roof of the tent. Brett jumped at the sudden sound and, after a chuckle, responded, "I smuggled a sudoku book in my waterproof bag, and I have a flashlight."

Ellie nodded, feeling herself relax once more. She spread out her bedroll and sleeping bag before lying down. The sounds of the storm lulled her off to sleep.

<hr>

Brett felt terrible. That was the only way to describe it. Cheerful, bubbly Ellie had just turned into a mushy mess in front of him. He didn't mind that she cried—in fact, he was glad she could get her emotions out—but he didn't like the reasons behind why she was upset.

It didn't take a rocket scientist to figure out what her stressors were. Their assignment had gone to shit, and some evil bird was after her. Not just after her. Trying to kidnap her.

His arm stung where its large talons had pierced his flesh. Sure, shifters had accelerated healing abilities, but as a sloth, his were faster than a regular human's but slower than the average shifter.

His arm throbbed as he tried to pry his sudoku book and flashlight out of his backpack. Brett felt dumb packing it at first, but now he was glad to have it. To take his mind off of what was going on. To help him focus.

The rain raged on the material roof of the tent, tattooing out a soothing rhythm as the darkness of night settled in around them. Thunder quaked the ground a few more times, following the lightning that ripped through the air, flashing a white light through the tent for a brief moment. Soon the rumbling and blinding light diminished as the storm moved on past their valley.

Ellie seemed to sleep through it all. Brett glanced up from his book every now and then to check on her. If she were still awake, she made no sign of it.

How would he protect her? It was difficult to keep his eyes on her every second. He supposed the real question was, *How does that hawk keep finding us?* His mind swirled with possibilities. It was as if it knew *exactly* where they were.

Brett pulled his knees into his chest, thinking. There had to be a tracking device on them. It was the only thing that made sense.

He opened his backpack, spilling all the contents onto the floor of the tent. He sorted through the food and supplies he'd carefully packed. The silver pouches reminded him that he had forgotten to eat dinner. After getting attacked, it was the last thing on his mind. He sifted through his change of clothes, finding his pocketknife buried in the middle of them. Nothing seemed out of the ordinary. There wasn't one single thing that shouldn't have been there. Next, he thumbed through the pages of his book. Nothing was tucked inside of it.

He didn't remember noticing anything that didn't

seem to belong on the tent. He inspected his bedroll next, finding nothing out of the ordinary. Brett wasn't even sure he would recognize a tracker if he found it—if it even existed—but he had to keep searching for one.

Once he decided all of his belongings were probably in the clear, he stared at Ellie. *Should I wake her? Or go through her bag without asking?* It felt like a violation of her privacy.

Brett glanced at the black waterproof watch that circled his wrist. It was almost ten o'clock. She had been sleeping for about three hours. He hoped it was the perfect length for a catnap.

"Ellie." He kept his voice soft, not wanting to startle her. Her shoulders raised and lowered as she took a deep breath, but aside from that, she did not stir. After a moment's hesitation, Brett reached out and gently shook her. "Ellie."

She groaned and rolled onto her back, throwing an arm over her eyes as if the beam from his flashlight was too strong for her to handle. "Is it time to switch?" She peered at him from under her limb before rubbing the sleep from her eyes.

"Not yet. I need you to do something for me."

"Okay." Ellie propped herself up on her elbows and yawned. Afterward, she raised a curious eyebrow.

Brett smiled at her. He couldn't help it. Her usual perfectly neat blonde bob stuck up in various places around her head. He had never seen her hair so messy. Not even after she removed her helmet earlier after they went for their unplanned swim.

"*What?*" she asked. The corners of her mouth turned up as she forced back a giggle.

"Nothing," he replied, momentarily forgetting why he woke her after seeing the cute, confused look on her face. And the way her messy hair was uncharacteristic of her, yet still charming. He remembered the way she felt in his arms when she'd cried earlier. The warmth of her body against him. The way his heart fluttered as she leaned into his chest.

Then it hit him like a pile of bricks, ripping him from his reverie as he remembered the search for a tracker. "No, not nothing," he corrected himself. "I was trying to figure out how the hawk seems to know where we are."

"And?" she asked, running a hand through her hair, taming it back down.

"There must be a tracker somewhere." He pointed back to the mess he'd made after going through his pack. "I couldn't find one in my stuff, so..."

"There may be something in my bag." Her brows furrowed together. She chewed on her bottom lip, staring at her sack as if it were some evil creature lying in wait. Ellie pulled it toward her, dumping out its contents.

"May I?" Brett asked before reaching for the empty bag.

"Knock yourself out," Ellie replied as she began inspecting her belongings and supplies.

Brett pulled the bookbag toward him, opening up the remaining zippered pockets. They were empty. He was about to drop the bag in defeat when he noticed a small tear in the lining of one of the smaller pockets in the front. A long, loose thread dangled where the seam split apart.

"What do you see?" Ellie asked quietly, noticing his change in demeanor.

"I am not sure yet," he admitted as he picked his flashlight up from his sleeping bag and put it in his mouth to light up the inside of the bag. He prodded a finger into the ripped lining of the pocket. At first, he felt nothing but soft material. Then he poked something small, flat, and solid. Something that didn't belong.

Brett pulled out the metal device. It looked almost like a round five-volt battery, thin and no larger than a nickel. A tiny bead of red sat at its center, blinking.

It felt as if they both held their breath at the same time. He looked to Ellie, watching the worry wash across her face. Her eyes grew wide, like two pale moons, as she stared at the device in his hand. Her eyes flicked up to his face. In the silence, she seemed to ask, *What do we do now*? Her lips pressed together in a thin line, forcing her to swallow her question.

Being unsure if it was just a tracking device or if it was also some sort of bug that could hear them,

Brett raised a finger to say, *Give me a minute.* He clutched the round disk in his fist and moved toward the door of the tent. Hearing the gentle patter of rain continuing on the roof, he grabbed his waterproof windbreaker from his pile of stuff on his sleeping bag and threw it on. Before unzipping the door and exiting the tent, he spotted his pocketknife in his pile of stuff. He picked it up and tossed it to Ellie, and gave her a wink before walking into the dismal night.

With the flashlight still gripped in his teeth, Brett could see the wet ground around him. Some small branches lay around, shaken loose from the recent wind of the storm. He found one about as thick as two of his fingers with a crack in it. He stuffed the tracker inside and shook the branch to make sure the device stayed put. Satisfied that it didn't fall out, he glanced back to the tent. Though he didn't want to leave Ellie for long, he knew it would be worth it if he could toss the tracker in the river and throw their pursuer off their scent.

Brett turned slowly around, scanning the trees around him for any movement. Shadows played around the trunks of the trees as his flashlight turned with him. It made it nearly impossible to tell if anyone lingered out there, watching them. He stood in silence for a moment, letting his sloth ears take over—his hearing ability being much better than his vision. He heard nothing but the sound of rain dripping in the trees and pattering on the mucky ground.

Satisfied that nothing seemed out of place, he walked away from the tent and toward the cliff's edge. He stepped as close as he dared before whipping the stick as far as he could into the air and toward the raging river below them. It was his hope that whoever was on the other end of the tracker thought they'd started moving again. If they did, then he and Ellie might have a restful night.

Which they needed. They were both beyond drained. Emotionally and physically.

Then Ellie's scream pierced the night.

9

Dr. Smith crouched in the damp ground of the forest. Water from the rain pooled beneath him. He would have been miserable save for the excitement that bubbled inside his brain. The shadow cat was in the glowing tent just twenty feet away. He watched the twinkle of the flashlight bob around within it. As soon as the light went out, he planned to make his move.

Since his hawk minion wasn't able to grab the girl or take out her companion, he had to make a move himself. Not only would the shifter add to his collection, but she would also be a valuable asset for his next set of experiments. A girl who could use dark matter within her to bend light. It was incredible. He *had* to find out how it worked!

As if a sign from above, the tent zipped open, and her male companion stepped into the rain, leaving the girl alone in the tent. The heavens smiled down on Dr. Smith. This was better than what he had planned! Instead of having to quietly kill her friend, he could sneak in while she was alone and snatch her up.

Dr. Smith was about to make his move when the male shifter suddenly stopped, inspecting the area around him with his light. Dr. Smith ducked behind the trunk of the large tree he was hiding behind, keeping as still as he could, hardly even breathing. The light of the flashlight lit the forest, shifting the shadows around him. Dr. Smith waited until the light left his area. He didn't dare move until the man left.

Soon darkness swept around Dr. Smith once more. He peeked out from around the trunk and watched the light recede toward the cliff and the waiting river below. The soft ground shifted beneath his sopping wet boots as he tore through the forest, toward the tent—and the shifter girl—that waited for him in the clearing. He knew his time was short. Soon the man would return. Dr. Smith had a limited time to grab the girl and make off with her.

Ellie heard quick footsteps approaching. She feared the worst. As the flap of the tent opened, she asked, "What's wrong?" The form silently crept into the tent. "Where's the flashlight?"

As she asked, she knew the answer. He didn't have a flashlight because he wasn't Brett. Her heightened senses alerted her to danger. This man *smelled* different from Brett.

Ellie screamed as loud as she could to warn Brett, wherever he was. She hoped he heard. As her yell broke through the still of the night, the stranger lunged at her. Ellie tried to kick, but she was still inside her sleeping bag. Instead, her foot slid off of the man's leg and shot toward the edge of the tent, kicking out one of the poles instead. The material fell around them. Ellie felt the wet of the rain kiss her through the fabric. It clung to her exposed skin and face. She felt like she was drowning, being dragged under by a damp sail of a ship.

Hands wrapped around her ankles. Ellie was still bound by the sleeping bag. The man dragged her. She was thrust into a mucky puddle of water outside. Her hand tightly clutched the pocketknife Brett had left her. She straightened her back defiantly, "You want me, come get me!" she shouted, opening the blade under the cover of night. Ellie struggled against the sleeping bag, trying to kick it off as it absorbed the rainwater that surrounded her.

Fooled into thinking she was stuck, the man lunged for her once more. She allowed him to pounce, letting him think he had the upper hand as she sank the blade into his side.

The man screamed in her ear. Ellie thought of all

the times she'd screamed in captivity as they experimented on her. She remembered how they laughed at her as they strapped her to the hospital bed. Ellie took the rage built up inside of her after months of that. Seeing all their cruel faces, knowing they did not view her as human. She was nothing more to them than an object. Something to be owned or possessed.

This man was no different. Her abilities were something this evil scientist wanted to master, to claim as his own.

No one would do that to her again, make her feel like that again.

She ripped the blade out before sinking it in once more. And then another. She took no notice as her fingers slipped on the handle with the next thrust, slick from blood. The blade nipped into her fingers as well as the flesh of the man.

"Ellie!" Brett's panicked voice ripped her from her mental anguish, bringing her back to the heavy body sputtering on top of her. Soon she was free from the weight as Brett flipped the man off of her, flooding his pale face with the beam of the flashlight. The assailant's eyes were open and hollow, non-reflective, all wrong.

Ellie sucked in quickly, about to drive the blade into him once more just in case. Brett caught her wrist. "He's dead, Ellie."

She looked up to Brett, finally feeling the cold

sting of the rain on her flesh. The cool fingers of water droplets traced multiple lines down her spine as they ran down her back. Ellie collapsed back into the mud with a *splat*. Her arms flailed out in exhaustion. Droplets clung to her eyelashes, blurring her vision, as she stared up at the black sky. She felt like the last person left in the world, frozen in pain, isolated in her anger. All alone.

Then a gentle hand pulled her up, pressing her into his warm body. Brett cupped her head in his hand, stroking her hair.

"I'm here," he reminded her, pulling her out of the mental darkness. "You're not alone, Ellie."

She melted into him, letting his words tickle her ear and send a tingling electricity down her neck, through her body, toward her heart. Heating her from the inside out.

Brett brushed her matted hair off her face. She leaned her cheek into his palm, drinking in his scent. Ellie tilted her chin up, inviting him closer. Brett's soft lips brushed hers, as if asking her if it was okay. Ellie covered his mouth with hers in answer. Her body tingled in response as she flitted her tongue around his, feeling the heat of his body mingle with her own.

"We have to get away from here," she said, breaking the kiss the moment she remembered their situation. She didn't dare look at the motionless form on the ground nearby. She'd done what she needed to do. That stranger had been after her, and she had to save herself.

"Yes, we do," Brett agreed. "I don't think there's any point in trying to salvage the tent." He pointed the beam of the flashlight to reveal their soggy mess of a tent, filling up with water, mud, and debris from the forest.

"I don't think we should go very far in the dark and rain," Ellie said with a sigh. "We could easily get turned around and lost or twist our ankles on uneven ground. Not to mention any wild animals that might be out there."

"Maybe we can sleep in the trees tonight," Brett suggested, looking up at the lush canopy above them.

Ellie glanced over her shoulder at the body. She didn't know how she could sleep after killing someone.

Brett put a hand over her eyes. "Don't think about it right now. We will rest up tonight if we can and tell Grayson about it tomorrow when we get to our extraction point."

Ellie nodded as Brett helped her to her feet and freed her from the sleeping bag. It dripped from his fingers as he picked it up. "It must weigh thirty pounds," he said with a huff. "Should I hang it up?"

Ellie raised an eyebrow glancing around them at the rain falling and the water dripping from the trees. "I don't think it can get any drier, but I don't think it could get any wetter, either."

Brett walked toward the nearest tree and hung the sleeping bag up anyway.

"Let's try to fix the tent if we can," he suggested.

He and Ellie struggled for about fifteen minutes before deciding it was a lost cause at this point. The sopping mess fought against them, and the poles refused to cooperate. The tent collapsed, rain flooded it, and they accepted the fact that their attempts were in vain.

"Your hand." Brett pointed the beam of the light at her, and Ellie saw red dripping into the mud.

"The blade slipped," she explained. "I'd forgotten all about the wound, thanks to all the adrenaline surging through me."

"Let's patch you up. Otherwise, your shifter healing won't kick in as quickly."

They inspected the cuts in the dim light. They didn't appear too deep, but the blood flow wasn't slowing. As she looked at it, the sting of the wounds throbbed through her hand. It was as if not seeing it made it unreal somehow.

"I'll try to find the med kit," Brett stated before fighting with the opening of the tent. The wet fabric clung to his body as he entered. Ellie tried her best to help prop the roof of their former shelter so Brett could find what he was searching for.

Brett eventually hobbled out of the blob that used to be their tent, clutching the flashlight and med kit.

He ushered Ellie over to the tall maple tree next to the towering pine, helping her out of the rain.

"Can you hold this with your good hand?" he asked, flipping the flashlight around so she could grab the handle.

"Yeah," Ellie replied. Her voice was soft, sounding almost alien to her ears. The shock was subsiding, and she was beginning to feel again. Pain seared through her fingers as an ache spread through her body. Her shoulders were tense after all the paddling, and her thighs burned from the hike. Her hand shook slightly as she held it out for Brett to inspect. Both her body and mind were exhausted.

His gentle fingers dabbed at her wound with gauze. She tried not to wince as he applied the antiseptic goo.

"I guess it's time to try sleeping in the tree," Ellie mused, looking up into the welcoming branches. She smiled at Brett as he finished taking care of the slices on her hands.

"After you," he said, propping the med kit up against the trunk of the tree and gesturing toward the branches.

Ellie nodded as Brett turned around, giving her privacy to remove her clothes and shift. Her body morphed around her, shrinking and changing until Ellie became the black cat she had come to love. Rain dampened her fur, and the mud squished between her tiny toes. She hoped that she didn't undo everything Brett had done to clean out her wound, but they needed to sleep, and this was their best option.

After a brief head-to-tail shake, Ellie ran up the trunk of the large tree that sheltered them, sinking her claws into it as she scrambled up its trunk. Her wounded paw stung with the climb, but she didn't feel that she had made it any worse. She kept close to the trunk until she found a suitable bough higher up to lie on. The bark was damp in places, but the leaves around her kept most of the moisture of the rain out.

Branches beneath her shook gently as Brett—in sloth form—made his way up the tree to join her. She'd always thought sloths were incredibly slow-moving, and while he did move carefully and at a languid pace, it didn't take him long to make it up to her. His claws hooked on the branch nearest her. His shaggy, brown fur ruffled around him as he got comfortable, hugging the giant trunk.

Exhaustion threatened to shut her eyes, but she kept them trained on Brett. She watched his eyes slowly close and his head drop as he drifted off to sleep. Soon she joined him, feeling a sense of safety wash over her.

10

———

The next day greeted them with chirping birds and a sleepy sun that hung low in the sky. The rain had ceased. Now a lazy fog swirled in the valley around them, blanketing the trees in grey and white. Brett opened his eyes after a stretch and a yawn to see Ellie carefully balanced on the large bough. Her head rested on her crossed front paws. She looked so peaceful. He didn't want to wake her. Not yet anyway.

He used his hooked claws to climb down the tree trunk to check out the damage to their camp below. It was slow going, but he was far more coordinated in his sloth form. And the thought of descending from the tree naked in human form was cringeworthy. Brett didn't even want to imagine how that would feel on his bare skin and nether region.

As he reached the soggy ground, Brett kept his

eyes averted from the direction of the dead man. Instead, he headed toward their tent. His skin tingled and itched as his fur receded, turning back into hair. The bones of his limbs popped and cracked as they lengthened. Soon Brett was in human form, reaching for the clothes that he'd neatly piled on one of the tree limbs above him. They were still soaking wet, but he figured he needed something on before he assessed the damage to their camp.

He fought with the tent poles once more, succeeding in propping up a lopsided enclosure. It was better than they'd accomplished last night. Water rolled off the fabric in tiny rivers. Brett gritted his teeth. It would be a miracle if anything within was still dry.

Brett was amazed to find that while the bottom of his bookbag was soaked, the clothes near the top weren't that bad. He changed into the dry garments and pulled out Ellie's bag. She wasn't as lucky. Her side of the tent was the wettest. Brett hung up what he could in the tree and laid an outfit out on a dry, sunny patch of a rock outcropping.

After Brett had everything hanging out to dry, he ripped open a granola bar for breakfast. He'd sat down on a rock when he heard a *plunk*. Ellie had jumped out of the tree. She stretched out her front legs with a yawn before hunching her back up. Her blue eyes seemed to glow behind the black fur. She peered up at him, blinking in the sunlight.

"I just laid everything out, but I doubt any of it is dry yet," Brett explained before taking a bite of his food. Cat Ellie sauntered over to him, weaving once through his legs before she stopped. He realized she was facing the direction of the dead man.

"I guess you didn't decide to ignore it, like I did," he said, finally making himself look in that direction.

Ellie ran forward to the empty spot where the body had been the night before.

Brett peered around. Aside from the wreck of a tent and hanging clothes in the trees, nothing else was in their clearing. The corpse was gone, and there weren't any footprints or drag marks in the still-wet ground to indicate that he'd been taken.

It was as if some creature plucked the body off the ground and flew away. Knowing the size of the hawk, Brett supposed that could have been what happened.

Brett looked up, heart pounding, searching for any sign of the hawk that chased them earlier. Nothing but regular-sized birds dotted the sky and sang on the nearby treetops.

Ellie's tail twitched in agitation as she sniffed the ground, as though conducting her own investigation. She let out a loud *meow* before peering up at the sky.

"I know," Brett replied. "I think the hawk took him too." He wasn't entirely sure that was what her cry meant, but it felt rude not to answer her.

She blinked back up at him with almond-shaped eyes, her pupils tiny slits in her blue irises under the bright light of the sun. Her tail continued to twitch impatiently, flicking dried dirt here and there.

"Do you want to see if you have any clothes dry enough to wear? Or should we wait a bit longer?" Brett asked her.

Ellie turned her attention back to the tree with the garments hanging in it before looking back to the skies.

"It makes me nervous too, thinking that bird is still out there," Brett admitted. He brought his hand up to the site of yesterday's wounds, which were now fully healed. Even so, he felt a phantom pain as he remembered the hawk swooping down and sinking its talons into his skin. He didn't want to see that creature ever again. Hopefully, it had slunk back to whatever lab it crawled out of. Maybe the man who'd tried to kidnap Ellie last night was its master, and it would move on, not having someone to tell it what to do.

Ellie *meowed* in agreement. After peeling her eyes away from the sky, she trotted off toward the tree where Brett had left her clothes. He found himself scanning the air above them in her absence.

But this time, it wasn't the hawk on his mind.

He brought his fingers to his lips, remembering the kiss that lingered there. Had Ellie kissed him because she had felt vulnerable under the circumstances and needed some affection? Had he taken advantage of the situation? He hoped she didn't view it that way. Brett didn't want the kiss to be a fluke of circumstances. He wanted their relationship to grow into something lasting.

Ellie was such a sweet girl. And under her bubbly exterior, she was tough as nails. He admired her perseverance, strength, smarts, and genuine niceness. His heart ached that Ellie was not only a rescued experiment but that she had to endure what had been happening to them on their trip. This was supposed to be a challenging—yet fun—assignment. True, they'd expected to be tested. But the stakes were way too high for Ellie. Someone was after her!

A gentle touch on his back brought him out of his thoughts. It was Ellie, smiling up at him, back in human form.

"How are you doing today?" he asked.

She bit her lip. The expression was so cute it took all Brett had in him not to kiss her again. "My clothes are a bit damp," she explained, tugging on them, "but I'll survive." She gave a weak smirk.

"I was asking about more than just the clothes." Brett didn't like that she seemed to be brushing off what had happened last night. He offered a slow smile, trying to put her at ease. To let her know that he supported her.

Her eyes looked distant as she turned back to the sky, scanning overhead. "I'll feel better when we get to the extraction point." She suddenly looked Brett over and smiled. "Maybe when this is done, you can take me out to dinner." Ellie gave his arm a playful squeeze before she trotted toward the tent. "Wanna help me pack up so we can get the hell outta here?" she called over her shoulder, her voice back to its usual bright timbre.

Brett's heart fluttered in his chest at her touch. And at her offer. *Dinner?* he thought. He couldn't wait to get them to safety so they could focus on each other.

Ellie didn't want to think about what had transpired last night. She *killed* someone. Or at least she thought she had. Was someone really dead if there was no evidence? Maybe they'd both been wrong. She couldn't remember checking the man's pulse. Maybe he'd shifted when they went up into the trees and then crawled off to heal.

The other thought was just as disturbing: that maybe someone or something had come while she and Brett were sleeping and taken the body. It was a miracle she and Brett weren't found. It was probably a good thing they'd taken shelter in the tree.

She couldn't decide which she'd rather believe—that she'd really killed someone and his body had been removed or that her attacker was still alive and out there.

In the end, she decided the best way to survive the

day would be to not think too hard about any of it. Be aware, be alert, but try to think of other things.

After she quickly ate, they were off weaving a path through the woods. Ellie wanted this nightmare of a camping trip to be over. She was sad it didn't turn out to be the fun excursion she was hoping for.

Brett asked to lead the rest of the way. Ellie watched his body as he moved ahead of her, clearing a path for them. Her body tingled as she thought of the kiss last night. She wished that she could relive that moment. His body pressed into hers. Her heart fluttering as hot passion built up in her core. Their lips meeting, soft and tender. His warm body wrapping around her. The…

Ellie slammed into the back of Brett, not realizing that he had stopped. She lost her balance and tripped on a root. The ground was rising up to meet her— more like she was crashing toward it. Brett effortlessly spun around, catching her in his strong arms.

She looked into his warm hazel eyes as he cradled her in his arms. He smiled down at her. The whole world melted away, and it was just the two of them in each other's arms.

Brett put her back on her feet but kept her gaze. It spread a tingling warmth throughout her body, sending butterflies floating in her stomach. Nothing else mattered but this moment. Not the assignment they were probably going to fail, not the man who'd tried to kidnap her and disappeared. Just her and

Brett. His hot fingers caressed her shoulders. It ignited a passion in her that she didn't know was there.

She needed this. Needed a chance to completely forget everything else for a moment and focus on the urges she'd had toward Brett for some time now.

A flame of desire licked at her body, tumbling down her spine until it pooled wetness in her loins. She leaned in, pressing her lips to his. They were soft and hot. His taste was intoxicating when she slipped her tongue inside his open lips. Their bodies entwined in a dance. Brett pulled away to leave a trail of hot kisses down her neck. His breath sent shivers down her arms.

Ellie shrugged off her backpack before it pulled her to the ground. Exhaustion nipped at her muscles, yet her body was so needy. It yearned for his touch. Her shadows danced off of her in small waves as her excitement built. They tingled the surface of her skin before leaving her body. Every sensation lit a new fire that grew her desire, burning deep inside her.

As if sensing her need, Brett cupped the back of her head before kissing her deeply once more. Ellie pulled back to remove her shirt. She wanted his scent all over her body. Wanted to feel his flesh pressed against her, to be as close to Brett as possible.

His wandering lips left another trail of kisses down her neck. After each one, a blossom of fiery passion grew within her core. Brett paused for a moment, nibbling on her collarbone. She leaned into the trunk of the tree behind her, her knees threatening to give out. Brett moved seamlessly with her, as if they were one being, connected by desire.

His tongue roamed in lazy circles over her flesh, inching closer to her racing heart. Ellie thought for sure he could feel it beating fiercely in her chest. He nipped at one of her breasts after freeing it from her bra. She grabbed a fistful of his hair, keeping his face close to her body, not wanting to lose any contact. His deft hands meandered over the flesh of her abdomen. They sent a trail of goosebumps down her upper arms.

Each sensation was pure pleasure. It was as if she had never felt the touch of another being in her entire life. True, Ellie had gaps in her memory from the experimentation and initial kidnapping to the lab that unfortunately became her home, but this was different. His touch satiated her. She *knew* that she had never experienced that before.

Brett paused, taking a step back to remove his own shirt. Ellie's eyes inspected every inch of his chiseled chest. Before she could reach out to caress his sculpted body, he laid his shirt on the forest floor as a makeshift bed for her. As he peeled her off of the tree, Ellie realized how the bark had been painfully digging into her back. She was so consumed by his touch that she paid no notice.

Brett set her down on his shirt, shielding her from

the dirt and leaves of the woods around them. Ellie lay down, inhaling all the scents around her. The deep smell of the earth and the musky scent of Brett and his arousal.

She had almost forgotten the heightened senses of shifters. That was another thing she had struggled to get used to after being only human for so long. Not only could she see the bulge of Brett's manhood against his pants, but she scented it. The sensation was indescribable. It was as if her former human senses were only capable of using five colors in the crayon box when twenty-four really existed. And now Ellie could use the full palette. At times, it was overwhelming. But at times like this, it was intoxicating.

The warm summer air flirted with her bare skin as Brett peeled off her pants and moist panties. She bared herself to him, opening her legs. Without hesitation, Brett dove in, lapping at the moisture between her thighs. Ellie nearly came at the sensation. His tongue explored her sex, pulsing in and out of her before swirling around her nub. He sucked at it gently, caressing her sensitive skin with his mouth.

The pressure within her was building at each stroke of his tongue, each suckle. She needed him deep within her. Right now.

"I need your cock," Ellie blurted out before realizing the thought was in her mind.

Brett obeyed. His erection sprang free as he

removed his pants. He was ready for her. Ellie reached up as he knelt down, pulling him down. His lips found her hungry mouth as he lengthened out and pressed his manhood into the apex between her thighs. He slid it along her channel without entering, teasing her. The smooth skin of his head felt amazing against her sex. She felt that she would burst. Her climax was building.

Without warning, he slid his shaft inside of her. A cry of pleasure slipped from Ellie's mouth as he filled her. Her pussy sucked at him, drawing him in deeper as her muscles pulsed around his sex. Her hips tilted, giving him deeper access to her core. She felt every inch of him as he slid in and out, graceful and passionate. His hungry lips sealed over hers.

Her breath quickened as she erupted around him. Again. And again.

He buried his face in her neck, his warm breath tickling her skin as his cock pulsed within her, spilling his seed. Its hot nectar dripped down her thigh as she held his body close to hers. She felt his heartbeat through his skin, tattooing a rhythm against hers.

His scent mingled with hers. Ellie didn't want to release him. She wanted to hold on to the comfort of him being inside of her forever. She protested with a groan as his manhood exited her body. He kissed the tip of her nose before standing, offering her a hand to help her up. She reached out, feeling drained. Her legs were jelly beneath her as she stood, struggling to find her clothing, which was strewn around their love nest. Brett giggled, plucking her bra out of a nearby tree. She snatched it from his hands, erupting into laughter herself. Ellie hoped this feeling would never end. As Brett smiled back at her, she hoped he felt the same way.

11

Brett's fingers were laced through Ellie's as the path evened out, and they no longer struggled to trudge downhill. They swapped stories of their lives. It pained him to hear how many gaps Ellie had in her memory. He could not even fathom what that must be like. Or how she managed to keep a bright disposition most of the time. It was a miracle that Ellie went through what she did and was still a beautiful person on the other side.

"I'm trying hard not to be a broken person," she blurted out after Brett told Ellie that he admired her bubbly personality. Her eyes seemed distant as she looked away to the line of minty-green pines in the distance.

"We're all different, Ellie, but no one is broken. You went through something," he clarified. It broke his heart to hear her say she felt defective. "Something terrible," he added, hoping she didn't think he minimized her experience. He could not imagine what she and the other rescued experiments had endured. It sickened him that they were used as lab rats.

Ellie gave him a weak smile and rolled her eyes. "It was fucked up for sure. But some days I just want to stay in bed… or cry."

"That's okay. It means you're healing. And look at all you have accomplished!"

"What do you mean?" She stopped walking and turned to him. Her brow raised as if she genuinely didn't know.

"You've had to handle not only transforming into a shifter but being okay with the fact that we exist. I'm sure that wasn't easy, but here you are, a FUC cadet, in a program designed to help other shifters."

Ellie rolled her eyes again and laughed as if dismissing what he said. "Yeah, but… I just know what it felt like to be lost, and I want to help others that feel that way. To be their beacon of hope. To pull them from the hells they may be living." He looked into her beautiful blue eyes. She seemed so far away. Probably thinking back to living in a lab.

"I think you'll be really good at that," Brett said. "I may have been born a shifter, and I couldn't even imagine what you and others have gone through…"

He paused, trying to find the right words. "But I know what it feels like to feel lost and what it feels like to have you there to help." He sighed, thinking about how judged he felt being a computer nerd at the academy. "I have felt like such an outsider as a cadet. I suck at the obstacle course. This outdoors stuff is all new to me."

"But you've done wonderfully!" Ellie exclaimed. "And being a FUC agent isn't about how well your aim is or how fast you can run. There's a place for everyone whose heart is in it"—Ellie laid a hand on his chest—"and yours is. You're a genuine, thoughtful, and caring person, and FUC is lucky to have agents like you."

Pride blossomed inside of him. He'd never thought that someone as well trained as Ellie would ever see value in him as an agent—or a person. "You really think so?"

Ellie nodded as a bright smile spread across her face. It melted all of Brett's insecurities.

"Now," Ellie said, turning to the path before them, "let's finish this assignment!"

The red, glowing ball of the sun was teetering on the edge of the mountains in the distance as they neared the extraction point. They were hours past when they were supposed to be there, but at least they'd made it. Ellie sighed in relief. With all this time outdoors, Ellie couldn't wait to go back to her dorm and shower. Although she didn't want to admit it, she secretly enjoyed the chance to finally dig holes in the ground to go to the bathroom and bury it. It gave her immense satisfaction. It was a thought she never imagined she would have.

A tall figure paced in the distance, stopping when they cleared the edge of the trees and neared the awaiting vehicle to take them back to WANC. Grayson turned toward them, hands on his hips. "It's about time you made it. We already sent the bus back with the others, and we were about to send out a search party for you two. Where's your raft?"

"Uhh…" Brett started, as though he didn't know how to begin telling Grayson that the raft was the least of their concerns.

"We… well…" Ellie, too, wondered how to explain it all.

Brett cut in. "A hawk came out of nowhere and grabbed Ellie from the raft."

"Not a normal hawk, a big one, likely a shifter." Ellie nodded, trying to swallow the fear she didn't allow herself to feel at the moment. "It flew off with me, but I was able to scratch the shit out of it, so it dropped me."

"What?" Grayson's mouth dropped. "You were *attacked?*"

"Yes, sir," Ellie quickly replied.

"But saved yourself."

"Yes. I made sure I would have a soft landing before I did so. I was able to time it so I fell into the branches of a tree."

"But you found each other?" Grayson looked between Ellie and Brett as he absorbed their tale.

"I pulled the raft over where Ellie and I had planned to rest," Brett explained. "I figured if I stayed in the planned location, she would meet me there. I waited a while and then finally saw her on the other side of the river. I paddled over to pick her up."

"Right." Ellie nodded. "But then we lost the raft in the next set of rapids."

"All right," Grayson said, rubbing his forehead with his hand. "Uh, well, sounds like you two appropriately assessed the situation and got out of harm's way. The parameters of the assignment did not include an enemy attack, but you two proved that you can appropriately change your plan accordingly. Now"—he reached into his pocket and pulled out his phone—"I'm going to have to call Director Cooper and inform her of this incident so we can try to find this hawk."

"Sir, wait. There's more." Tears stung Ellie's eyes as the weight of what happened next pressed against her heart. "I think I killed someone."

"What happened?" Grayson blanched. He shook his head, blinking rapidly and taking a few deep breaths. Clearly, the survivalist training instructor hadn't been prepared to handle *this*.

"It was my fault," Brett started. "I left the tent for a second—"

"It wasn't your fault!" Ellie cut him off. "You were taking care of the tracker that *you* had the brilliant idea to look for in the first place!"

"Tracker?" Grayson asked. His fingers were on his temple now, as if he were trying to hold in all of this information.

Ellie's chest swelled with pride thinking about how Brett was able to piece it all together. "We couldn't figure out how the hawk kept finding us. It actually swooped down and attacked Brett when we were in a clearing in the woods. Brett figured out that there must be a tracker on us. He found it. But when he went to send it floating down the river, a man entered the tent and grabbed me." Tears swelled in her eyes, spilling down her cheeks. She began to shake and couldn't continue.

Brett stepped over, putting his arm around her before filling in what she was unable to recount. "I had left Ellie my pocketknife just in case. And she stabbed the man in self-defense."

"Okay." Grayson nodded slowly. "Do you think you can show us on the map where you left the body so FUCN'A can send in a retrieval team?"

"Noooo..." Brett said, drawing out the word. "Uh,

not because I don't remember the location but because the body was gone in the morning."

"Which is why I said I *think* I killed someone. We don't know…" Ellie trailed off, unable to find the right words.

"Dr. Smith," FUCN'A director, Alyce Cooper, said from the speakerphone, which Ellie hadn't even realized Grayson had turned on. "His name was Dr. Smith, and we were after him for a while. His body mysteriously turned up this morning. Grayson, get these cadets back to WANC, ASAP."

"Will do." Grayson hung up his phone and replaced it in his pocket. He pressed his lips together, deep in thought. "I am glad you two are safe. What an ordeal. Come on, let's get you back." He turned toward the waiting truck.

"Did we pass?" Ellie asked, choking back her tears. "Even though we were late getting back?"

Grayson turned back to the pair, eyeing them up. "I'd say you both exceeded expectations. This was to be a pretend assignment. Cadets were to prove that they could survive in the wilderness when in the field but with no real danger occurring. However, you two had to deal with a crisis as true FUC agents."

A wide smile broke across his face. Ellie was taken aback. Instructor Grayson hardly showed that much emotion in class.

"You both deserve top scores for resourcefulness

and your ability to change your plan when necessary."

Ellie reached out and squeezed Brett's hand. She couldn't have done it without him. He pulled her in for a hug, wrapping his arms tight around her. The assignment was over, but everything else between them was just beginning.

12

———

The pub near FUCN'A was hopping, being a Friday and near the end of the semester. Many cadets were eager for a break. Ellie and Brett met up with Paige and FUC Agent Jake Park—who Paige had been dating for almost a year—for burgers and drinks.

"I just don't know how you were able to keep Ellie calm in a boat," Paige said after gulping down a swig of beer. "She was so flustered when she first explained this assignment to me."

Brett felt the warmth of a blush creep up his cheeks. "I think Ellie calmed herself down. I deserve no credit for that." He smiled at her. She returned the look before pressing her lips to his. Brett was glad that with the semester ending, they had more time for each other.

"Brett did give me some confidence," Ellie admitted with a shrug.

Jake smiled at them both. "I hear we will be coworkers soon. I am always looking forward to new agents."

Ellie's shadows were practically bouncing off of her in excitement. "Being a cadet was overwhelming at times, but I feel so accomplished and can't wait to start the next chapter of my life. And making a difference for others."

Brett smiled at her. He was so proud of her. "I'll just be a computer guy."

"There's no such thing," Jake said. "Without tech agents, the field agents couldn't do our jobs. We're all on the same team with the same goals."

Brett loved the support that he felt from his friends. He always felt less than when next to field agents like Jake. But Jake was right. While Brett's work was more behind the scenes, he would work just as hard as anyone else at FUC.

Ellie squeezed his hand before raising her glass. "To teamwork!" The four of them clinked their glasses together as if making a promise. Brett was so grateful to be surrounded by good people. He looked forward to seeing Ellie each day. Their bond was stronger than anything he had ever known before. It was as if they were made for each other. They could agree to disagree when needed or could work together in any situation. He could face anything knowing that Ellie would be there to back him up, and he knew she felt the same.

Grayson opened the file on his desk. He didn't like it when his students came under attack. In their debriefing, Ellie and Brett fully explained their encounter with the red-tailed hawk shifter and Dr. Smith. The evil scientist had been accounted for when his body mysteriously showed up, but the giant bird was still at large. Grayson hated assignments left unfinished. And bad guys still at large.

He scrolled through the pictures of birds spotted at various labs that had been raided by FUC in the past couple of years, hoping to find clues as to who this hawk was. He'd already put in requests with ASS —the Avian Soaring Society—but they rarely enjoyed working with FUC. Which meant he couldn't rely on them to help him identify the attacker.

"I hear you're going back into the field," a familiar female voice cut in over his shoulder, smooth as velvet.

Grayson snapped his head toward the door, watching ASS Agent Cass Sparks float into his office on stiletto heels. *Those damn heels.* Good agents wore practical shoes, but not Agent Sparks. Though no one could say anything about it since she proved she easily balanced and maintained stealth in them. Still, it seemed she took being a peacock shifter too much to heart, feeling the need to flaunt herself like one.

Didn't she know it was only male peacocks who were flashy and colorful?

"What are you doing here, Sparks?" Grayson muttered, turning back to his file.

"What do you *think* I'm doing here? This is ASS business."

"The hell it is." He shook his head in protest. "They came after two of *my* students. I am hunting that rat with wings down."

"You're not off the case," Cass replied. "I'm just on it, too."

Grayson's eyes flicked back up to her. *Why me?* Where he was grit and steel, Cass was equally fluff and sparkles. Their styles were oil and water.

Cass brushed a red curl out of her face, putting it back in line with the others. The gems on her acrylic nails caught in the light with the motion of her hand. The corners of her red lips pulled back into a sly smile. "Did you hear me? I'm going with you."

Grayson raised an eyebrow, biting back the words he wanted to say. He and Cass on a team? He was surprised they hadn't spontaneously burst into flames being in the same room. After their last mission together, he was under the impression she wanted nothing more to do with him. "I thought—" he started.

"Forget about what I said in Toronto," Cass said, her voice husky as she perched on the corner of his desk, crossing one leg over the other and batting her long black lashes at Grayson. "We have a bird to fry."

The End

Or is it? Stay tuned for Grayson and Cass' mission, coming in Peacock and the Hound *by Scarlet Fox, releasing summer 2023!*

And there are more FUC Academy books from other authors coming your way!

To find out more about these books and more, visit worlds.EveLanglais.com or sign up for the EveL Worlds newsletter. If you haven't already downloaded the **free Academy intro** (written by Eve Langlais) make sure you grab it at worlds.evelanglais.com/wordpress/book/fucacademy1!

Taming the Tiger

After being rescued from experimentation at a lab, Paige wants nothing more than to get on with her life. What's more frustrating than trying to fill in the blanks of her memory is the annoying—yet sexy—FUC agent who is hell-bent on protecting her while finding those responsible for her condition. But this tiger is sick of being kept in a cage.

Troubling memories from Jake's past leave him obsessed with arresting those who held Paige in captivity. If his nagging desire to be closer to her didn't prevent him from spending all hours of the day on the case, Jake is sure he would have outfoxed the evil scientists by now. But something keeps leading him back to Paige.

Can Jake keep his focus long enough to find those responsible for the atrocities committed against Paige? Or will a major miscalculation allow them to find her and complete their experiment?

Out now on all platforms!

ABOUT THE AUTHOR

Scarlet Fox (aka B.L. Carroll) enjoys writing when she isn't at her day job. Creating romances is a fun challenge for her. Scarlet's alter ego loves writing mysteries and supernatural thrillers with a strong female lead.

Destigmatizing mental health and other internal struggles are recurring themes in her fiction. Other hobbies include painting, singing, or going for walks. Coffee is a necessity, as is reading. She lives in western New York with her fur babies and partner.

Website: scarletfoxauthor.wixsite.com

 facebook.com/ScarletFoxAuthor

www.ingramcontent.com/pod-product-compliance
Lightning Source LLC
Chambersburg PA
CBHW030329160726
47992CB00005B/2210